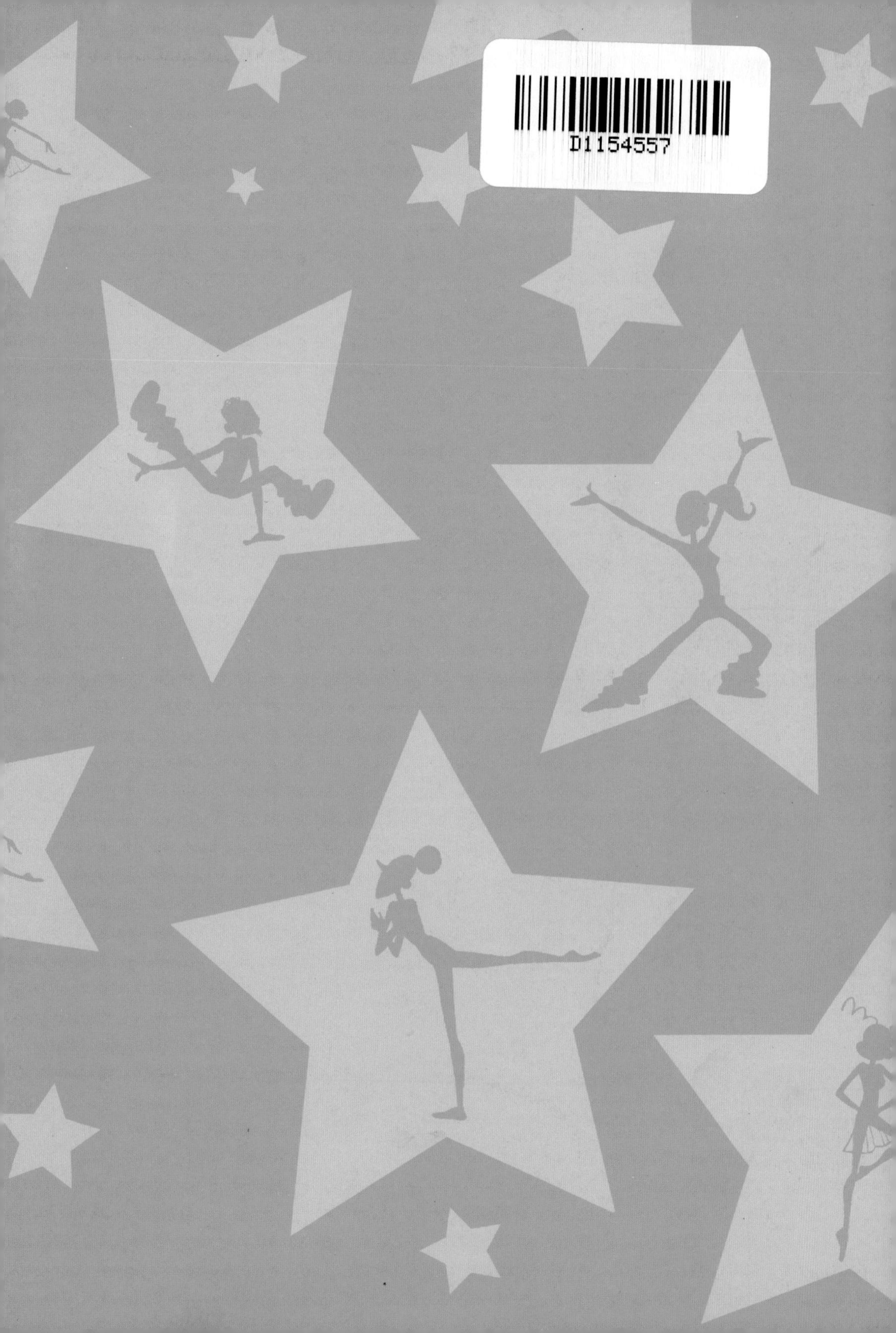

Dance Class

Crip • Art

Béka • Story

Maëla Cosson • Color

New York

Dance Class Graphic Novels Available from PAPERCUTZ

Béka and Crip
Dance Class
So, You Think You Can Hip-Hop?
PAPERCUTZ

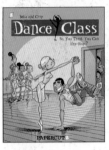

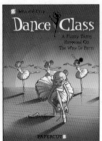

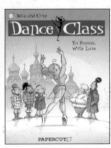

#1 "So, You Think You Can Hip-Hop?"

Béka and Crip
Dance Class
Romeos and Juliet
PAPERCUTZ

#2 "Romeos and Juliet"

Béka and Crip
Dance Class
African Folk Dance Fever
PAPERCUTZ

#3 "African Folk Dance Fever"

Béka and Crip
Dance Class
PAPERCUTZ

#4 "A Funny Thing Happened on the Way to Paris..."

Béka and Crip
Dance Class
To Russia, With Love
PAPERCUTZ

#5 "To Russia, With Love"

Béka and Crip
Dance Class
A Merry Olde Christmas
PAPERCUTZ

#6 "A Merry Olde Christmas"

Béka and Crip
Dance Class
School Night Fever
PAPERCUTZ

#7 "School Night Fever"

Béka and Crip
Dance Class
Snow White and the Seven Dwarves
PAPERCUTZ

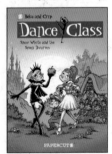

#8 "Snow White and the Seven Dwarves""

DANCE CLASS graphic novels are available for $10.99 only in hardcover, available from booksellers everywhere. You may also order online from Papercutz.com. Or call 1-800-886-1223, Monday through Friday, 9 - 5 EST. MC, Visa, and AmEx accepted. To order by mail, please add $4.00 for postage and handling for first book ordered, $1.00 for each additional book and make check payable to NBM Publishing. Send to: Papercutz, 160 Broadway, Suite 700, East Wing, New York, NY 10038.

DANCE CLASS graphic novels are also available digitally wherever e-books are sold.

Papercutz.com

Dance Class

DANCE CLASS #8
"Snow White and the Seven Dwarves"

Béka - Writer
Crip - Artist
Maëla Cosson - Colorist
Joe Johnson - Translation
Tom Orzechowski - Lettering
Alexander Lu - Editorial Intern
Beth Scorzato - Production Coordinator
Michael Petranek - Editor
Jim Salicrup
Editor-in-Chief

ISBN: 978-1-62991-057-4

Printed in China
November 2014 by New Era Printing LTD.
Unit C, 8/F Worldwide Centre
123 Chung Tau, Kowloon, Hong Kong

Papercutz books may be purchased for business or promotional use. For information on bulk purchases please contact Macmillan Corporate and Premium Sales Department at (800) 221-7945 x5442.

Distributed by Macmillan
First Papercutz Printing

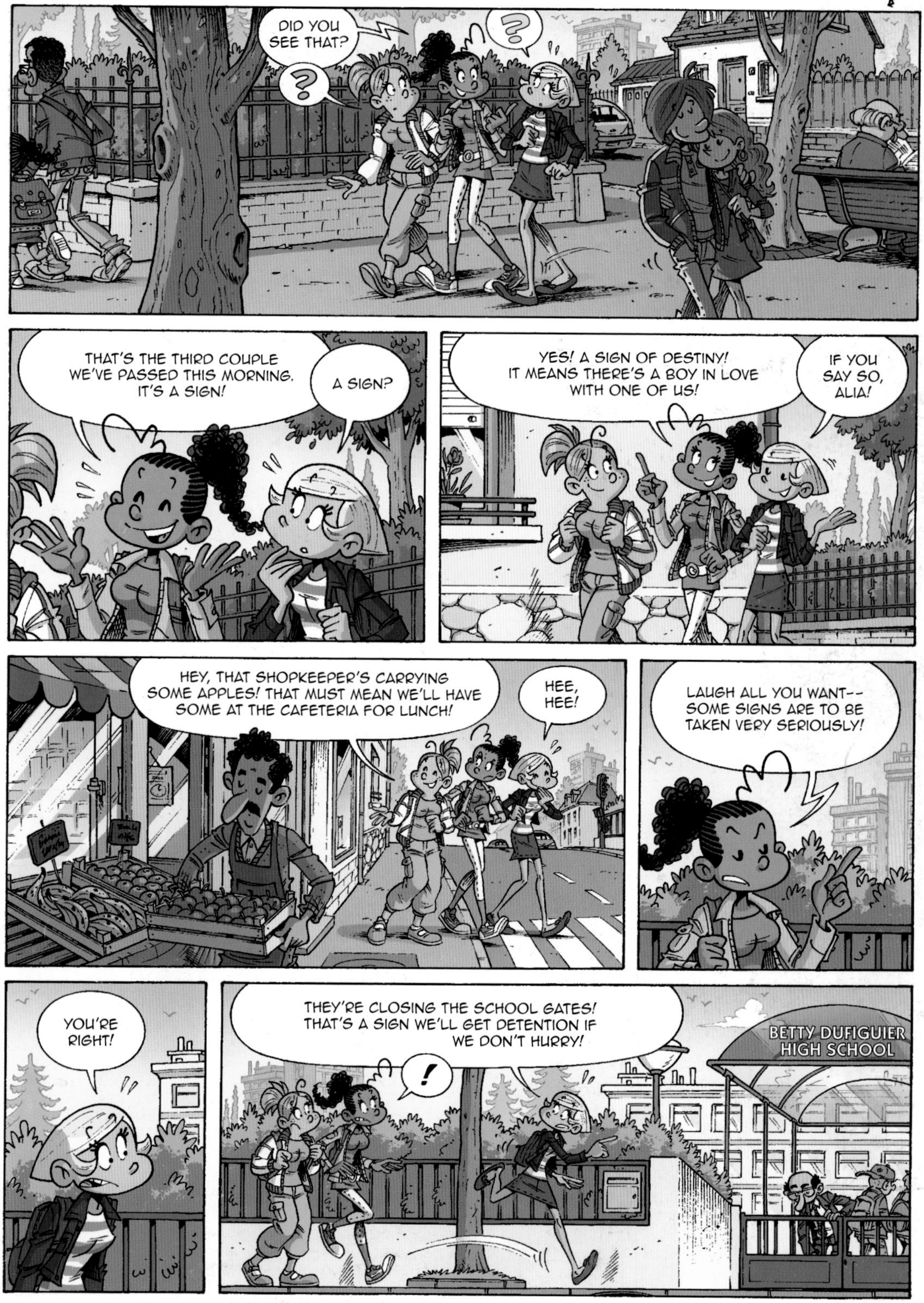
DID YOU SEE THAT?
?
?
THAT'S THE THIRD COUPLE WE'VE PASSED THIS MORNING. IT'S A SIGN!
A SIGN?
YES! A SIGN OF DESTINY! IT MEANS THERE'S A BOY IN LOVE WITH ONE OF US!
IF YOU SAY SO, ALIA!
HEY, THAT SHOPKEEPER'S CARRYING SOME APPLES! THAT MUST MEAN WE'LL HAVE SOME AT THE CAFETERIA FOR LUNCH!
HEE, HEE!
LAUGH ALL YOU WANT-- SOME SIGNS ARE TO BE TAKEN VERY SERIOUSLY!
YOU'RE RIGHT!
THEY'RE CLOSING THE SCHOOL GATES! THAT'S A SIGN WE'LL GET DETENTION IF WE DON'T HURRY!
!
BETTY DUFIGUIER HIGH SCHOOL

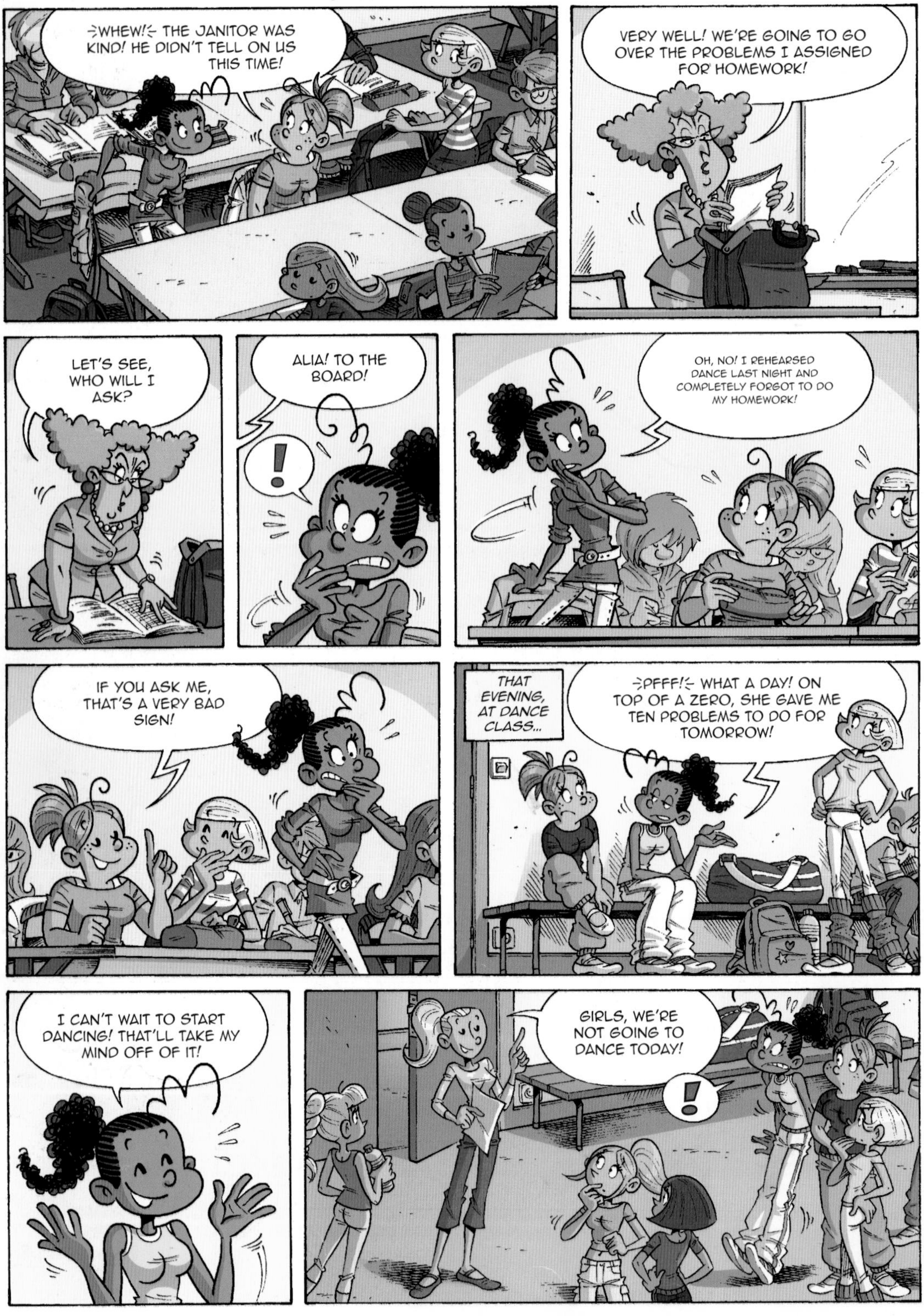

WHEW! THE JANITOR WAS KIND! HE DIDN'T TELL ON US THIS TIME!
VERY WELL! WE'RE GOING TO GO OVER THE PROBLEMS I ASSIGNED FOR HOMEWORK!
LET'S SEE, WHO WILL I ASK?
ALIA! TO THE BOARD!
!
OH, NO! I REHEARSED DANCE LAST NIGHT AND COMPLETELY FORGOT TO DO MY HOMEWORK!
IF YOU ASK ME, THAT'S A VERY BAD SIGN!
THAT EVENING, AT DANCE CLASS...
PFFF! WHAT A DAY! ON TOP OF A ZERO, SHE GAVE ME TEN PROBLEMS TO DO FOR TOMORROW!
I CAN'T WAIT TO START DANCING! THAT'LL TAKE MY MIND OFF OF IT!
GIRLS, WE'RE NOT GOING TO DANCE TODAY!
!

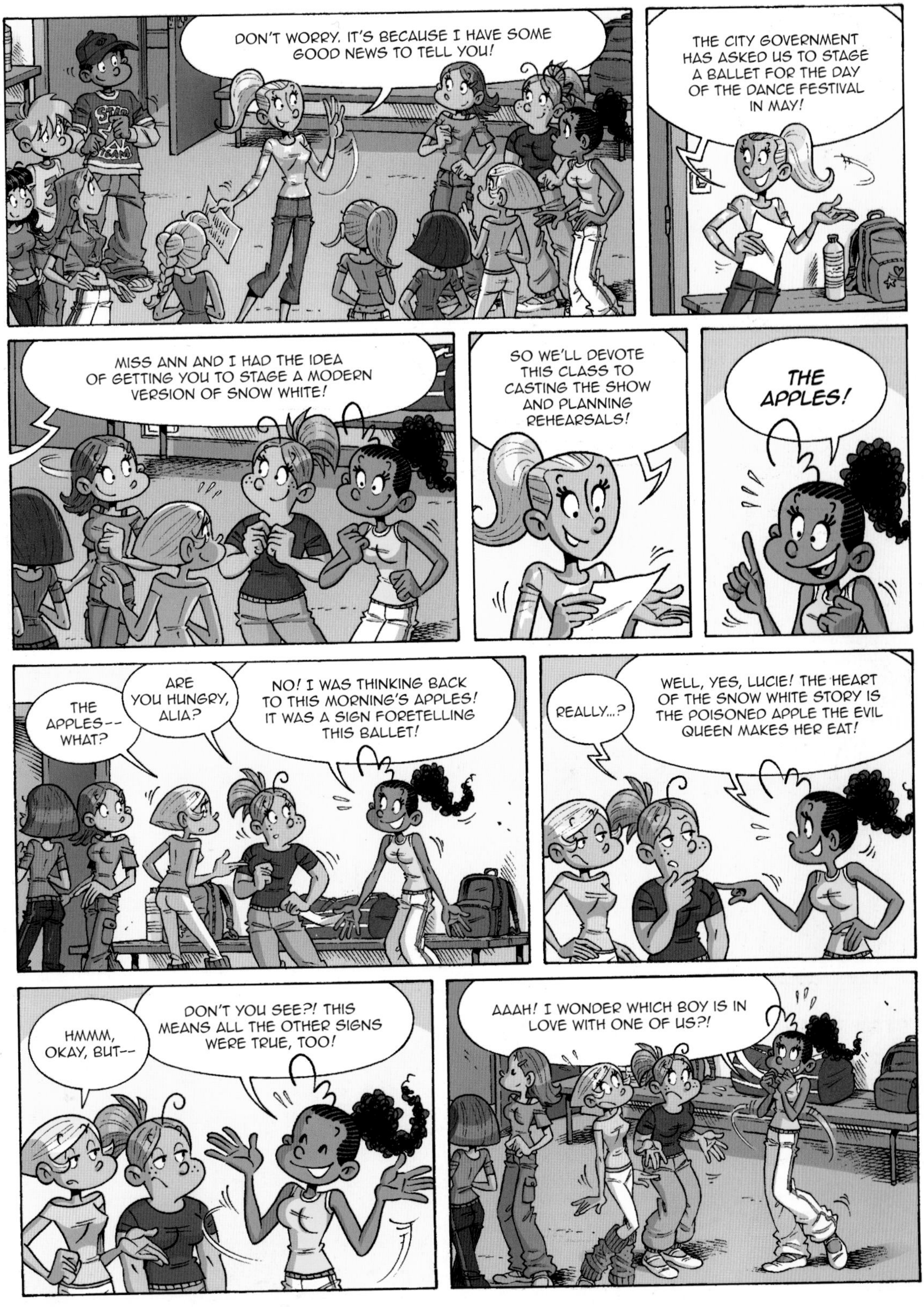
DON'T WORRY. IT'S BECAUSE I HAVE SOME GOOD NEWS TO TELL YOU!
THE CITY GOVERNMENT HAS ASKED US TO STAGE A BALLET FOR THE DAY OF THE DANCE FESTIVAL IN MAY!
MISS ANN AND I HAD THE IDEA OF GETTING YOU TO STAGE A MODERN VERSION OF SNOW WHITE!
SO WE'LL DEVOTE THIS CLASS TO CASTING THE SHOW AND PLANNING REHEARSALS!
THE APPLES!
THE APPLES-- WHAT?
ARE YOU HUNGRY, ALIA?
NO! I WAS THINKING BACK TO THIS MORNING'S APPLES! IT WAS A SIGN FORETELLING THIS BALLET!
REALLY...?
WELL, YES, LUCIE! THE HEART OF THE SNOW WHITE STORY IS THE POISONED APPLE THE EVIL QUEEN MAKES HER EAT!
HMMM, OKAY, BUT--
DON'T YOU SEE?! THIS MEANS ALL THE OTHER SIGNS WERE TRUE, TOO!
AAAH! I WONDER WHICH BOY IS IN LOVE WITH ONE OF US?!

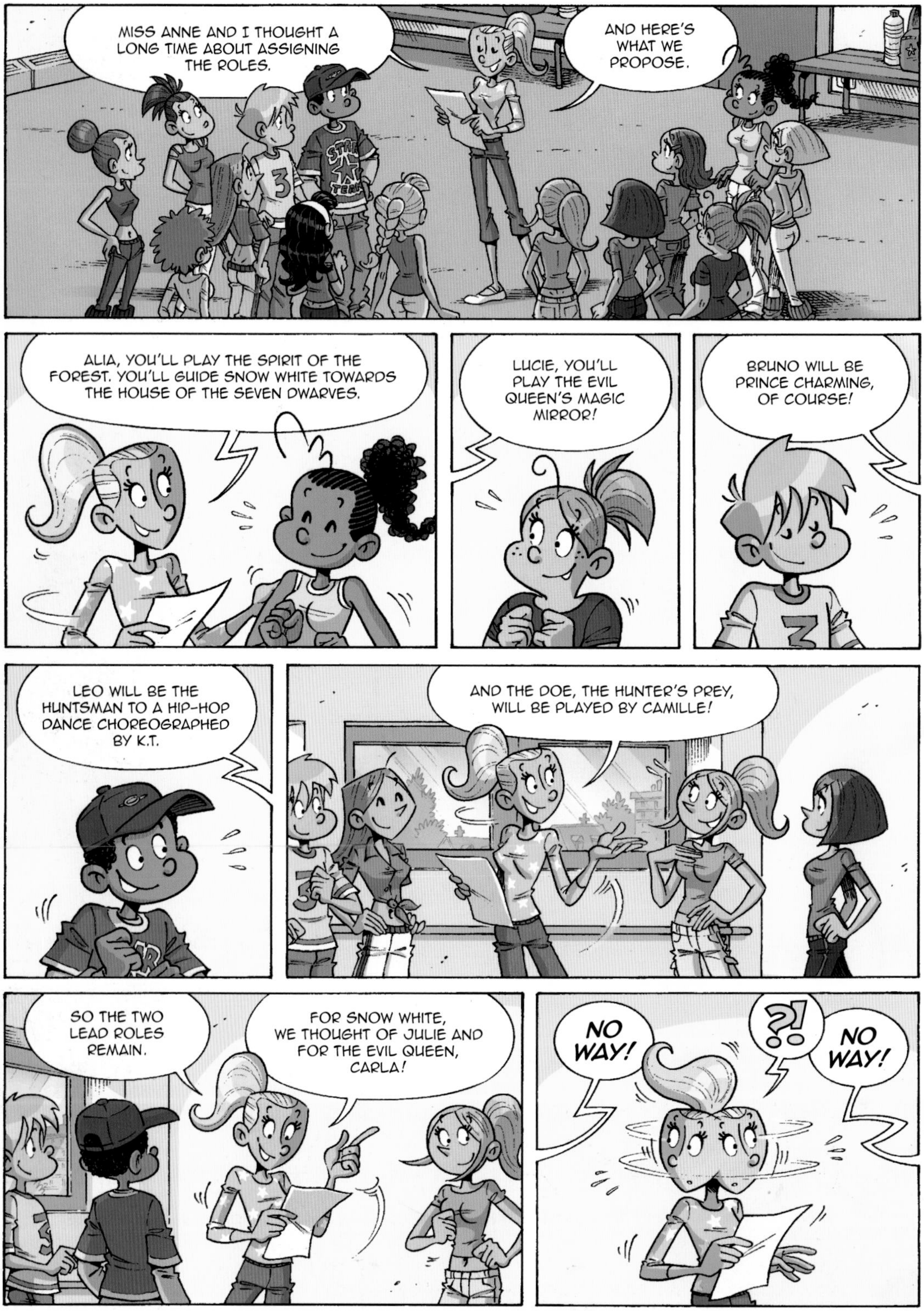
MISS ANNE AND I THOUGHT A LONG TIME ABOUT ASSIGNING THE ROLES.
AND HERE'S WHAT WE PROPOSE.
ALIA, YOU'LL PLAY THE SPIRIT OF THE FOREST. YOU'LL GUIDE SNOW WHITE TOWARDS THE HOUSE OF THE SEVEN DWARVES.
LUCIE, YOU'LL PLAY THE EVIL QUEEN'S MAGIC MIRROR!
BRUNO WILL BE PRINCE CHARMING, OF COURSE!
LEO WILL BE THE HUNTSMAN TO A HIP-HOP DANCE CHOREOGRAPHED BY K.T.
AND THE DOE, THE HUNTER'S PREY, WILL BE PLAYED BY CAMILLE!
SO THE TWO LEAD ROLES REMAIN.
FOR SNOW WHITE, WE THOUGHT OF JULIE AND FOR THE EVIL QUEEN, CARLA!
NO WAY!
?!
NO WAY!

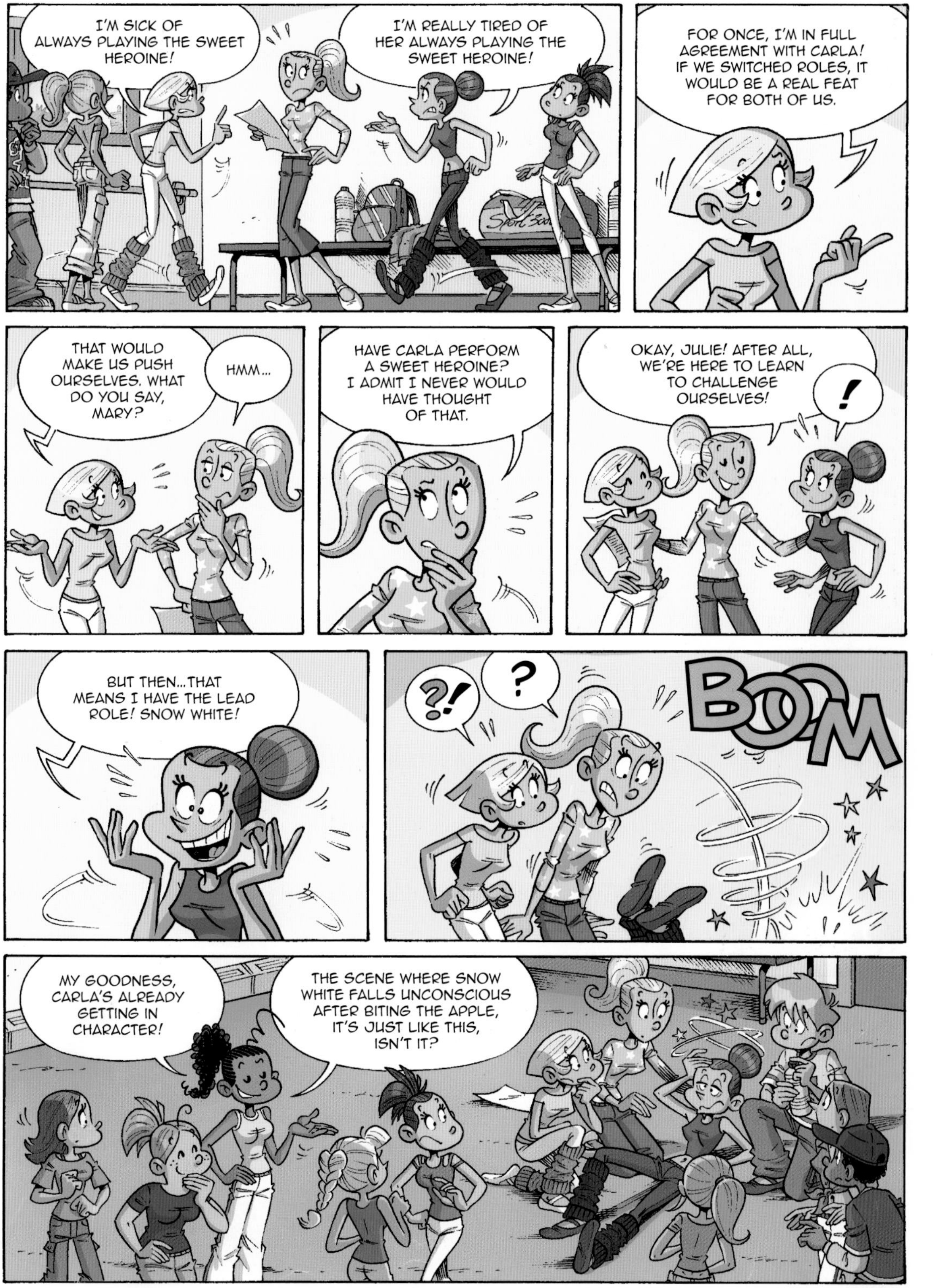
I'M SICK OF ALWAYS PLAYING THE SWEET HEROINE!
I'M REALLY TIRED OF HER ALWAYS PLAYING THE SWEET HEROINE!
FOR ONCE, I'M IN FULL AGREEMENT WITH CARLA! IF WE SWITCHED ROLES, IT WOULD BE A REAL FEAT FOR BOTH OF US.
THAT WOULD MAKE US PUSH OURSELVES. WHAT DO YOU SAY, MARY?
HMM...
HAVE CARLA PERFORM A SWEET HEROINE? I ADMIT I NEVER WOULD HAVE THOUGHT OF THAT.
OKAY, JULIE! AFTER ALL, WE'RE HERE TO LEARN TO CHALLENGE OURSELVES!
!
BUT THEN...THAT MEANS I HAVE THE LEAD ROLE! SNOW WHITE!
?!
?
BOOM
MY GOODNESS, CARLA'S ALREADY GETTING IN CHARACTER!
THE SCENE WHERE SNOW WHITE FALLS UNCONSCIOUS AFTER BITING THE APPLE, IT'S JUST LIKE THIS, ISN'T IT?

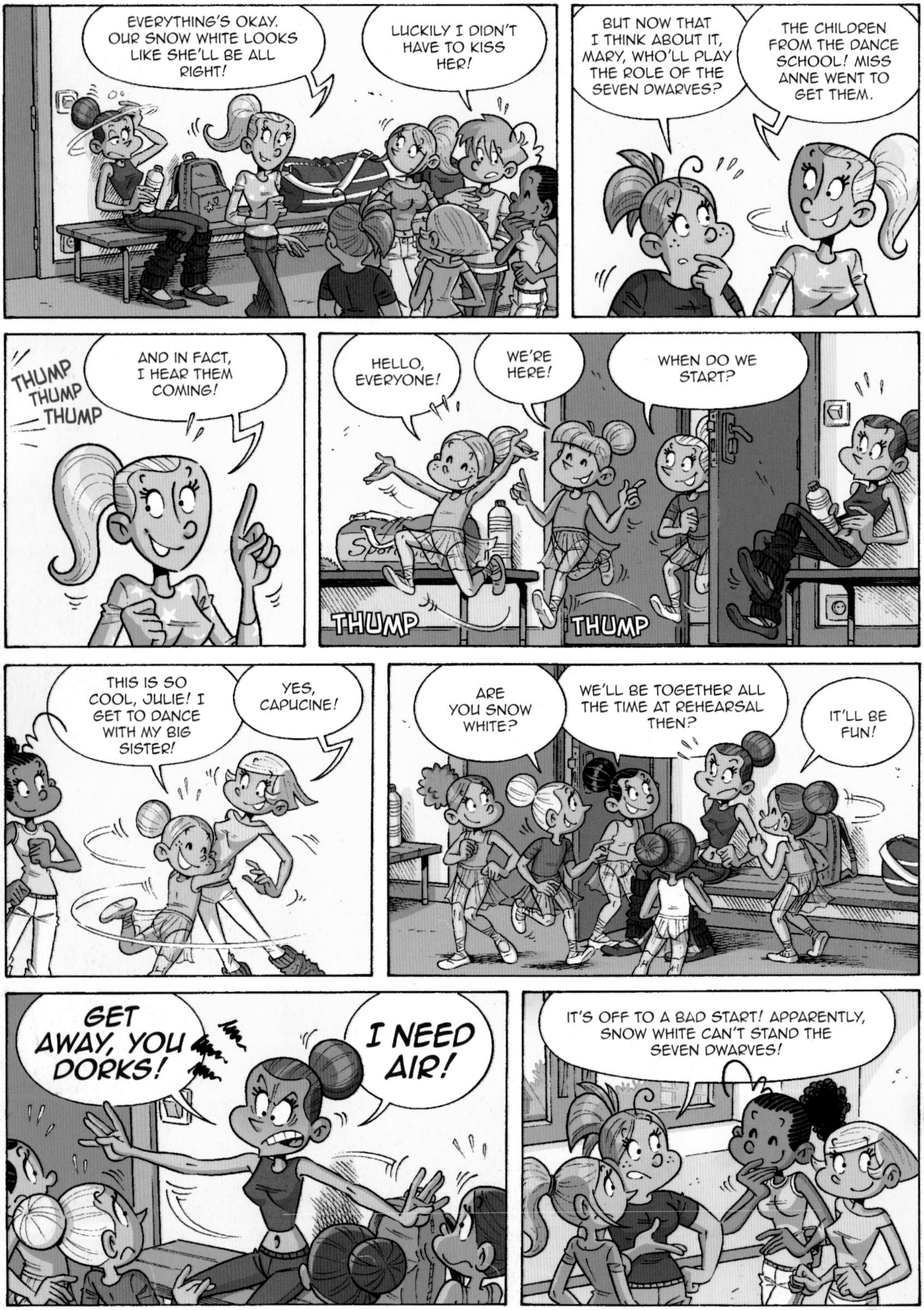
EVERYTHING'S OKAY. OUR SNOW WHITE LOOKS LIKE SHE'LL BE ALL RIGHT!
LUCKILY I DIDN'T HAVE TO KISS HER!
BUT NOW THAT I THINK ABOUT IT, MARY, WHO'LL PLAY THE ROLE OF THE SEVEN DWARVES?
THE CHILDREN FROM THE DANCE SCHOOL! MISS ANNE WENT TO GET THEM.
THUMP THUMP THUMP
AND IN FACT, I HEAR THEM COMING!
HELLO, EVERYONE!
WE'RE HERE!
WHEN DO WE START?
THUMP
THUMP
THIS IS SO COOL, JULIE! I GET TO DANCE WITH MY BIG SISTER!
YES, CAPUCINE!
ARE YOU SNOW WHITE?
WE'LL BE TOGETHER ALL THE TIME AT REHEARSAL THEN?
IT'LL BE FUN!
GET AWAY, YOU DORKS!
I NEED AIR!
IT'S OFF TO A BAD START! APPARENTLY, SNOW WHITE CAN'T STAND THE SEVEN DWARVES!

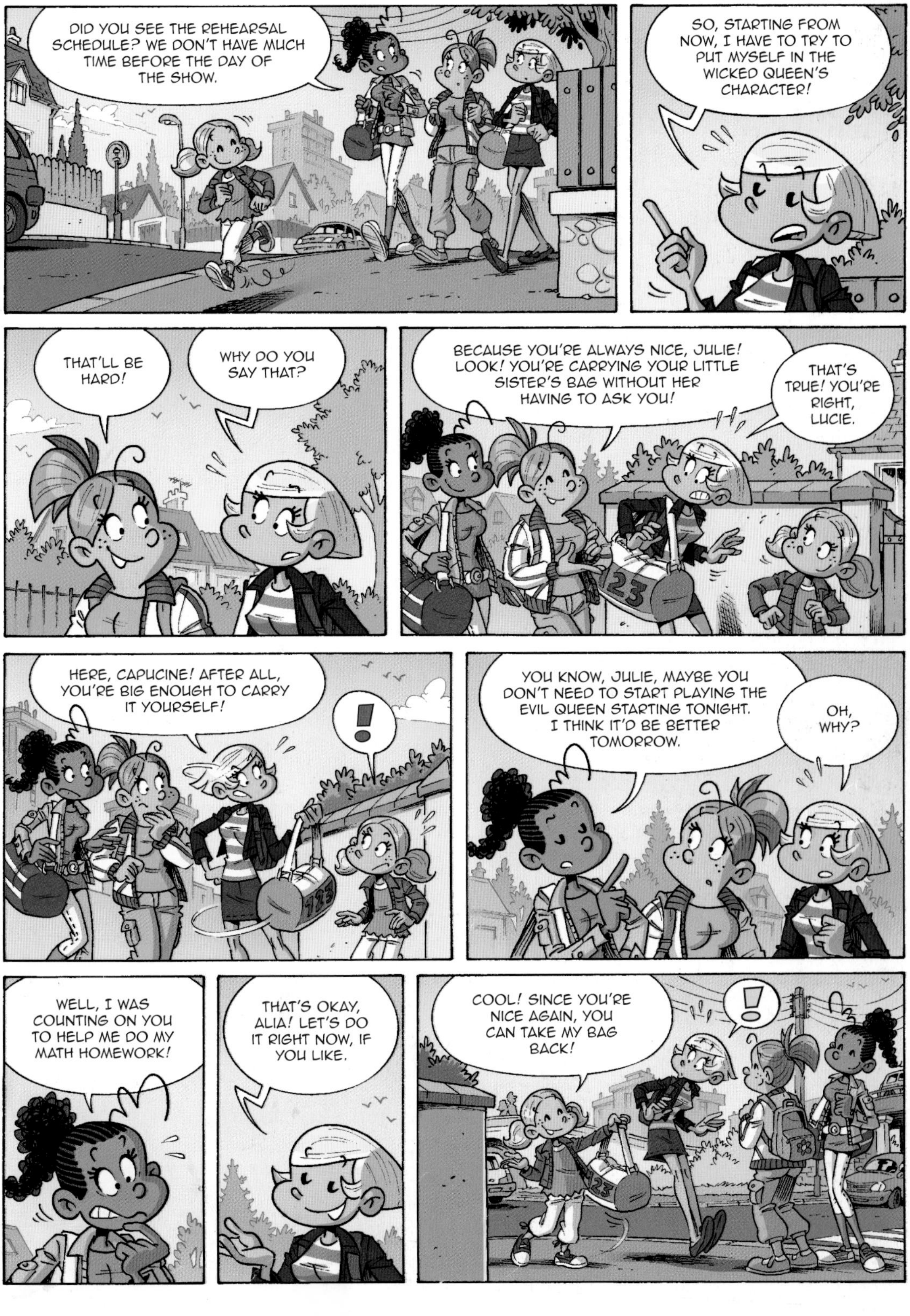
DID YOU SEE THE REHEARSAL SCHEDULE? WE DON'T HAVE MUCH TIME BEFORE THE DAY OF THE SHOW.
SO, STARTING FROM NOW, I HAVE TO TRY TO PUT MYSELF IN THE WICKED QUEEN'S CHARACTER!
THAT'LL BE HARD!
WHY DO YOU SAY THAT?
BECAUSE YOU'RE ALWAYS NICE, JULIE! LOOK! YOU'RE CARRYING YOUR LITTLE SISTER'S BAG WITHOUT HER HAVING TO ASK YOU!
THAT'S TRUE! YOU'RE RIGHT, LUCIE.
HERE, CAPUCINE! AFTER ALL, YOU'RE BIG ENOUGH TO CARRY IT YOURSELF!
!
YOU KNOW, JULIE, MAYBE YOU DON'T NEED TO START PLAYING THE EVIL QUEEN STARTING TONIGHT. I THINK IT'D BE BETTER TOMORROW.
OH, WHY?
WELL, I WAS COUNTING ON YOU TO HELP ME DO MY MATH HOMEWORK!
THAT'S OKAY, ALIA! LET'S DO IT RIGHT NOW, IF YOU LIKE.
COOL! SINCE YOU'RE NICE AGAIN, YOU CAN TAKE MY BAG BACK!
!

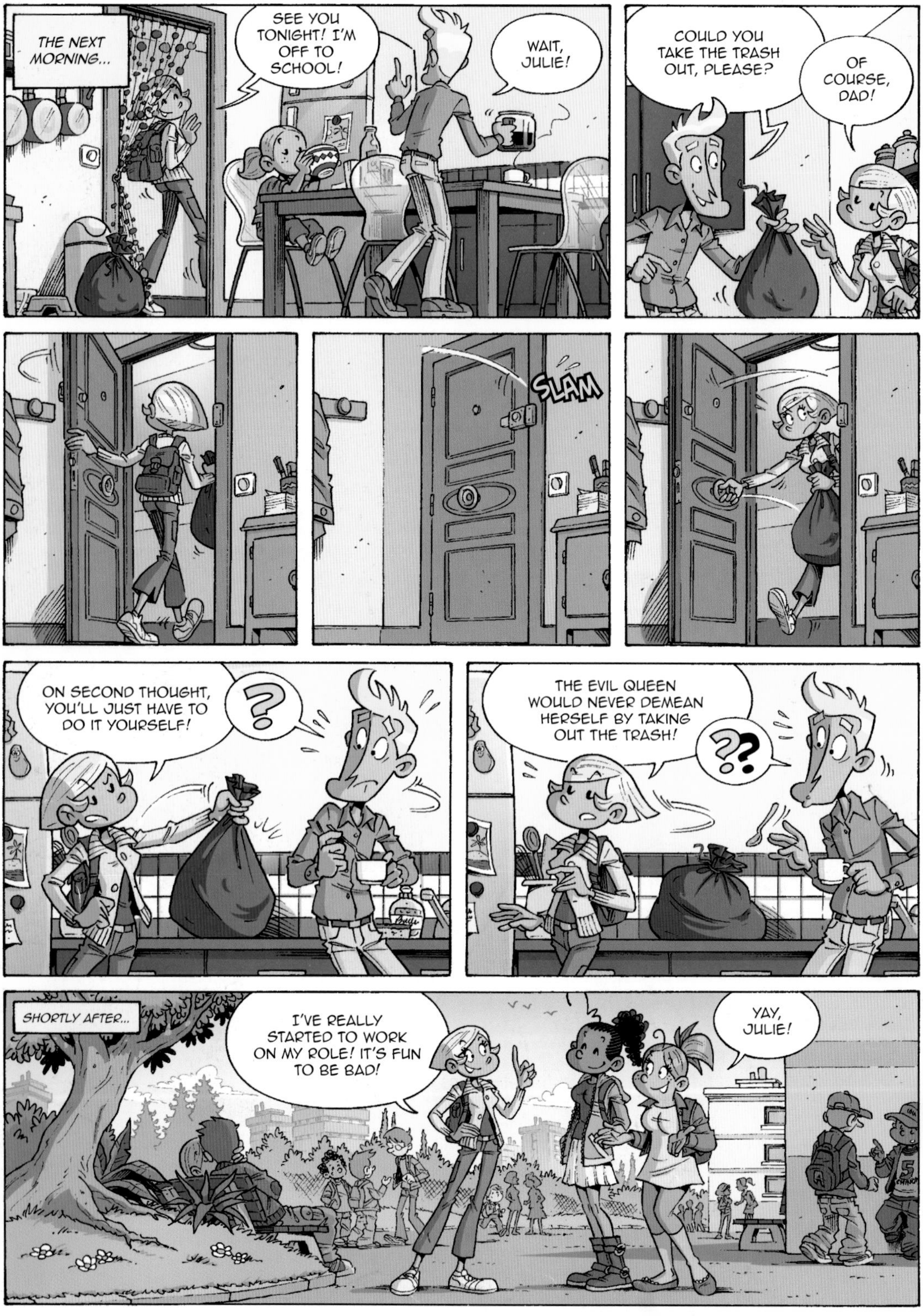
THE NEXT MORNING...
SEE YOU TONIGHT! I'M OFF TO SCHOOL!
WAIT, JULIE!
COULD YOU TAKE THE TRASH OUT, PLEASE?
OF COURSE, DAD!
SLAM
ON SECOND THOUGHT, YOU'LL JUST HAVE TO DO IT YOURSELF!
?
THE EVIL QUEEN WOULD NEVER DEMEAN HERSELF BY TAKING OUT THE TRASH!
??
SHORTLY AFTER...
I'VE REALLY STARTED TO WORK ON MY ROLE! IT'S FUN TO BE BAD!
YAY, JULIE!

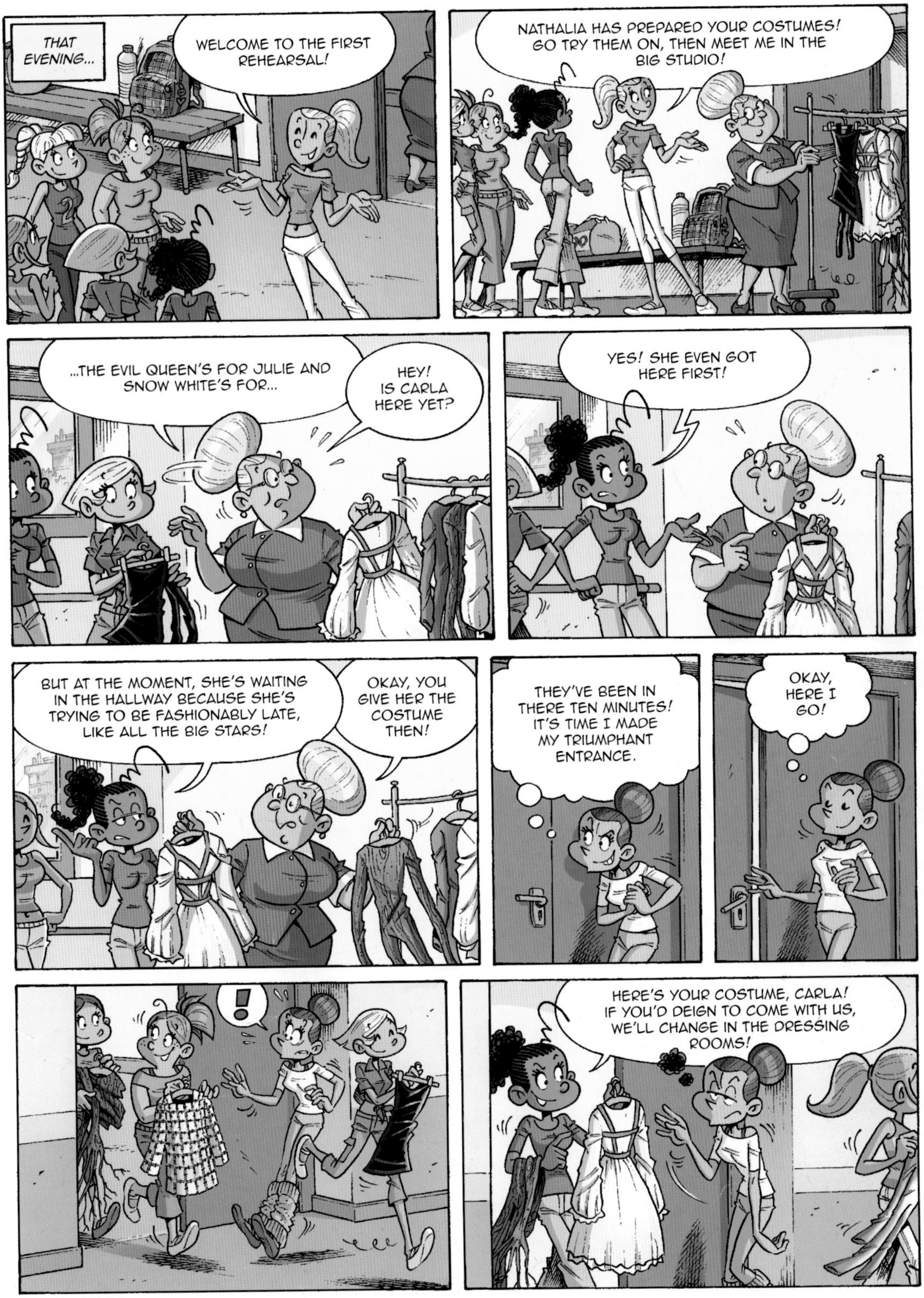
THAT EVENING...
WELCOME TO THE FIRST REHEARSAL!
NATHALIA HAS PREPARED YOUR COSTUMES! GO TRY THEM ON, THEN MEET ME IN THE BIG STUDIO!
...THE EVIL QUEEN'S FOR JULIE AND SNOW WHITE'S FOR...
HEY! IS CARLA HERE YET?
YES! SHE EVEN GOT HERE FIRST!
BUT AT THE MOMENT, SHE'S WAITING IN THE HALLWAY BECAUSE SHE'S TRYING TO BE FASHIONABLY LATE, LIKE ALL THE BIG STARS!
OKAY, YOU GIVE HER THE COSTUME THEN!
THEY'VE BEEN IN THERE TEN MINUTES! IT'S TIME I MADE MY TRIUMPHANT ENTRANCE.
OKAY, HERE I GO!
!
HERE'S YOUR COSTUME, CARLA! IF YOU'D DEIGN TO COME WITH US, WE'LL CHANGE IN THE DRESSING ROOMS!

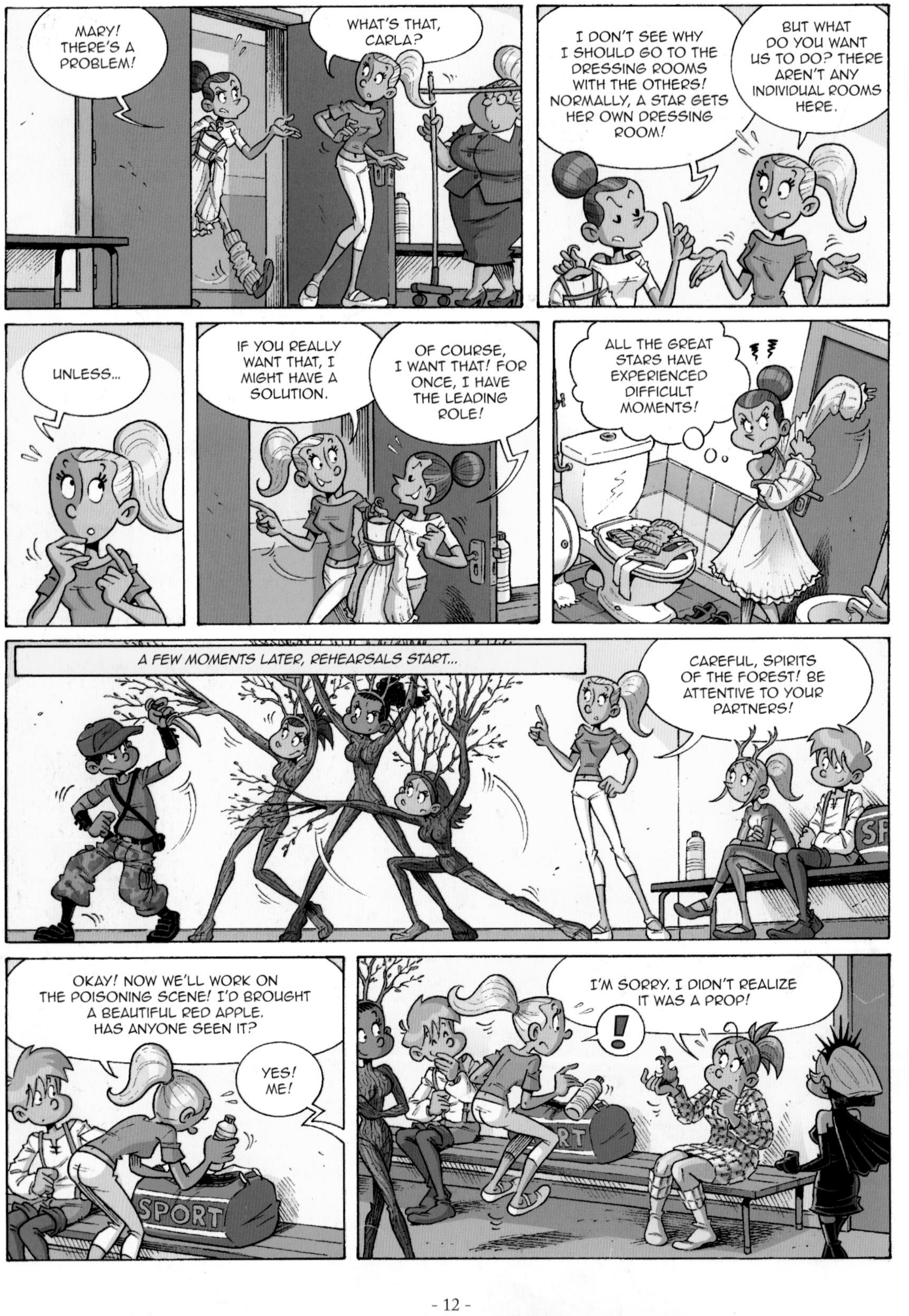
MARY! THERE'S A PROBLEM!
WHAT'S THAT, CARLA?
I DON'T SEE WHY I SHOULD GO TO THE DRESSING ROOMS WITH THE OTHERS! NORMALLY, A STAR GETS HER OWN DRESSING ROOM!
BUT WHAT DO YOU WANT US TO DO? THERE AREN'T ANY INDIVIDUAL ROOMS HERE.
UNLESS...
IF YOU REALLY WANT THAT, I MIGHT HAVE A SOLUTION.
OF COURSE, I WANT THAT! FOR ONCE, I HAVE THE LEADING ROLE!
ALL THE GREAT STARS HAVE EXPERIENCED DIFFICULT MOMENTS!
A FEW MOMENTS LATER, REHEARSALS START...
CAREFUL, SPIRITS OF THE FOREST! BE ATTENTIVE TO YOUR PARTNERS!
OKAY! NOW WE'LL WORK ON THE POISONING SCENE! I'D BROUGHT A BEAUTIFUL RED APPLE. HAS ANYONE SEEN IT?
YES! ME!
SPORT
I'M SORRY. I DIDN'T REALIZE IT WAS A PROP!
!

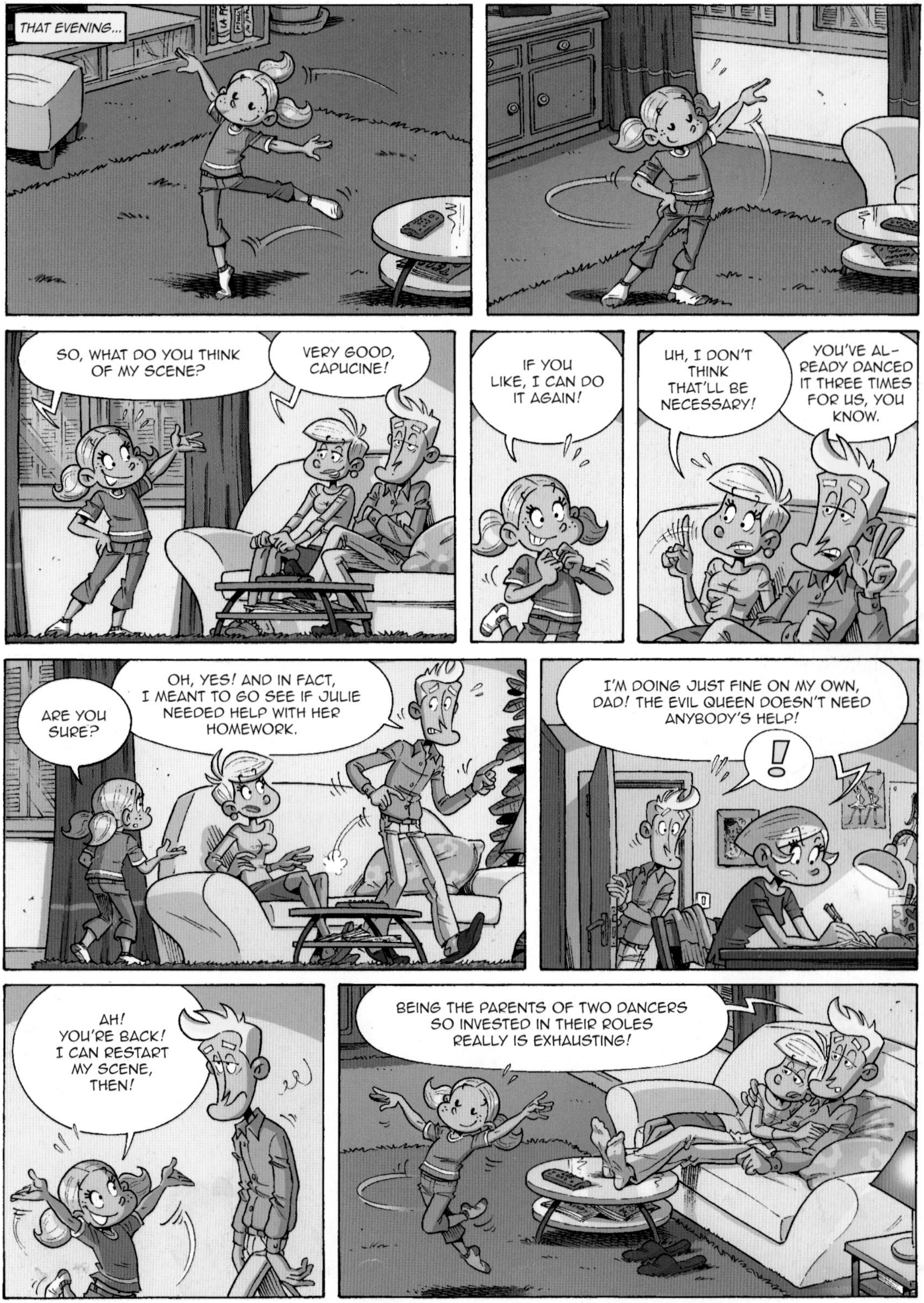
THAT EVENING...
SO, WHAT DO YOU THINK OF MY SCENE?
VERY GOOD, CAPUCINE!
IF YOU LIKE, I CAN DO IT AGAIN!
UH, I DON'T THINK THAT'LL BE NECESSARY!
YOU'VE AL-READY DANCED IT THREE TIMES FOR US, YOU KNOW.
ARE YOU SURE?
OH, YES! AND IN FACT, I MEANT TO GO SEE IF JULIE NEEDED HELP WITH HER HOMEWORK.
I'M DOING JUST FINE ON MY OWN, DAD! THE EVIL QUEEN DOESN'T NEED ANYBODY'S HELP!
!
AH! YOU'RE BACK! I CAN RESTART MY SCENE, THEN!
BEING THE PARENTS OF TWO DANCERS SO INVESTED IN THEIR ROLES REALLY IS EXHAUSTING!

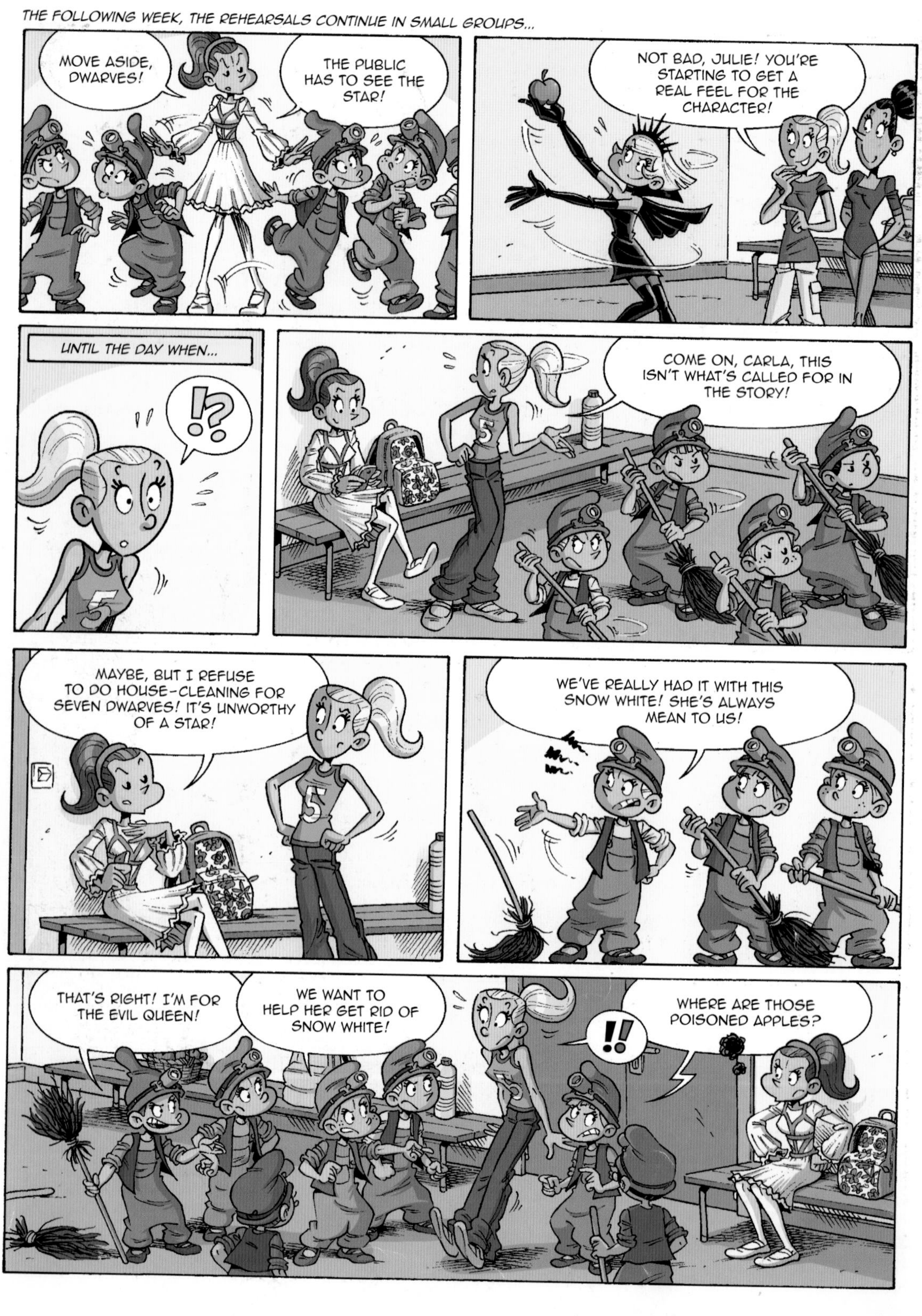
THE FOLLOWING WEEK, THE REHEARSALS CONTINUE IN SMALL GROUPS...
MOVE ASIDE, DWARVES!
THE PUBLIC HAS TO SEE THE STAR!
NOT BAD, JULIE! YOU'RE STARTING TO GET A REAL FEEL FOR THE CHARACTER!
UNTIL THE DAY WHEN...
!?
COME ON, CARLA, THIS ISN'T WHAT'S CALLED FOR IN THE STORY!
MAYBE, BUT I REFUSE TO DO HOUSE-CLEANING FOR SEVEN DWARVES! IT'S UNWORTHY OF A STAR!
WE'VE REALLY HAD IT WITH THIS SNOW WHITE! SHE'S ALWAYS MEAN TO US!
THAT'S RIGHT! I'M FOR THE EVIL QUEEN!
WE WANT TO HELP HER GET RID OF SNOW WHITE!
!!
WHERE ARE THOSE POISONED APPLES?

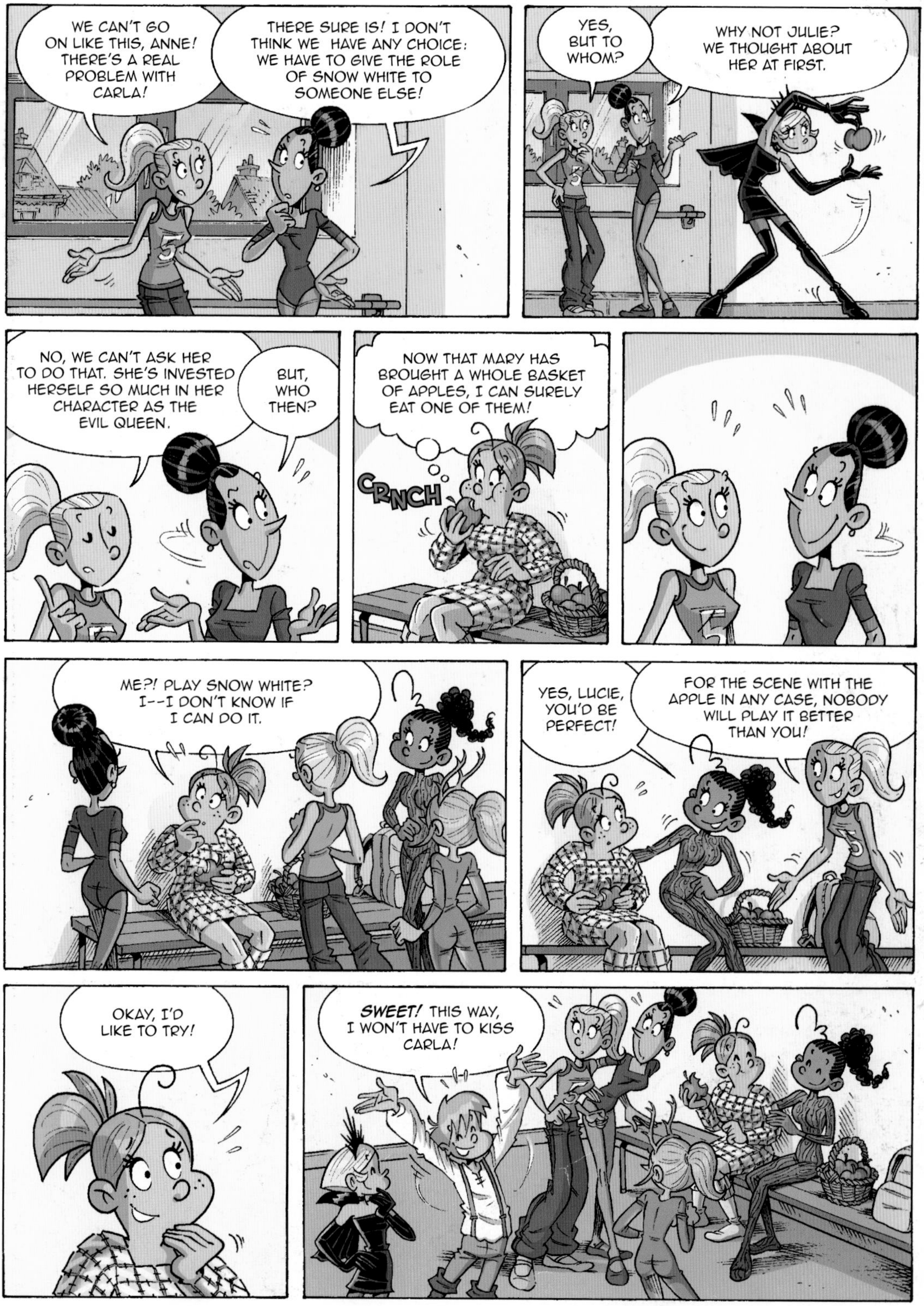
WE CAN'T GO ON LIKE THIS, ANNE! THERE'S A REAL PROBLEM WITH CARLA!
THERE SURE IS! I DON'T THINK WE HAVE ANY CHOICE: WE HAVE TO GIVE THE ROLE OF SNOW WHITE TO SOMEONE ELSE!
YES, BUT TO WHOM?
WHY NOT JULIE? WE THOUGHT ABOUT HER AT FIRST.
NO, WE CAN'T ASK HER TO DO THAT. SHE'S INVESTED HERSELF SO MUCH IN HER CHARACTER AS THE EVIL QUEEN.
BUT, WHO THEN?
NOW THAT MARY HAS BROUGHT A WHOLE BASKET OF APPLES, I CAN SURELY EAT ONE OF THEM!
CRNCH
ME?! PLAY SNOW WHITE? I--I DON'T KNOW IF I CAN DO IT.
YES, LUCIE, YOU'D BE PERFECT!
FOR THE SCENE WITH THE APPLE IN ANY CASE, NOBODY WILL PLAY IT BETTER THAN YOU!
OKAY, I'D LIKE TO TRY!
SWEET! THIS WAY, I WON'T HAVE TO KISS CARLA!

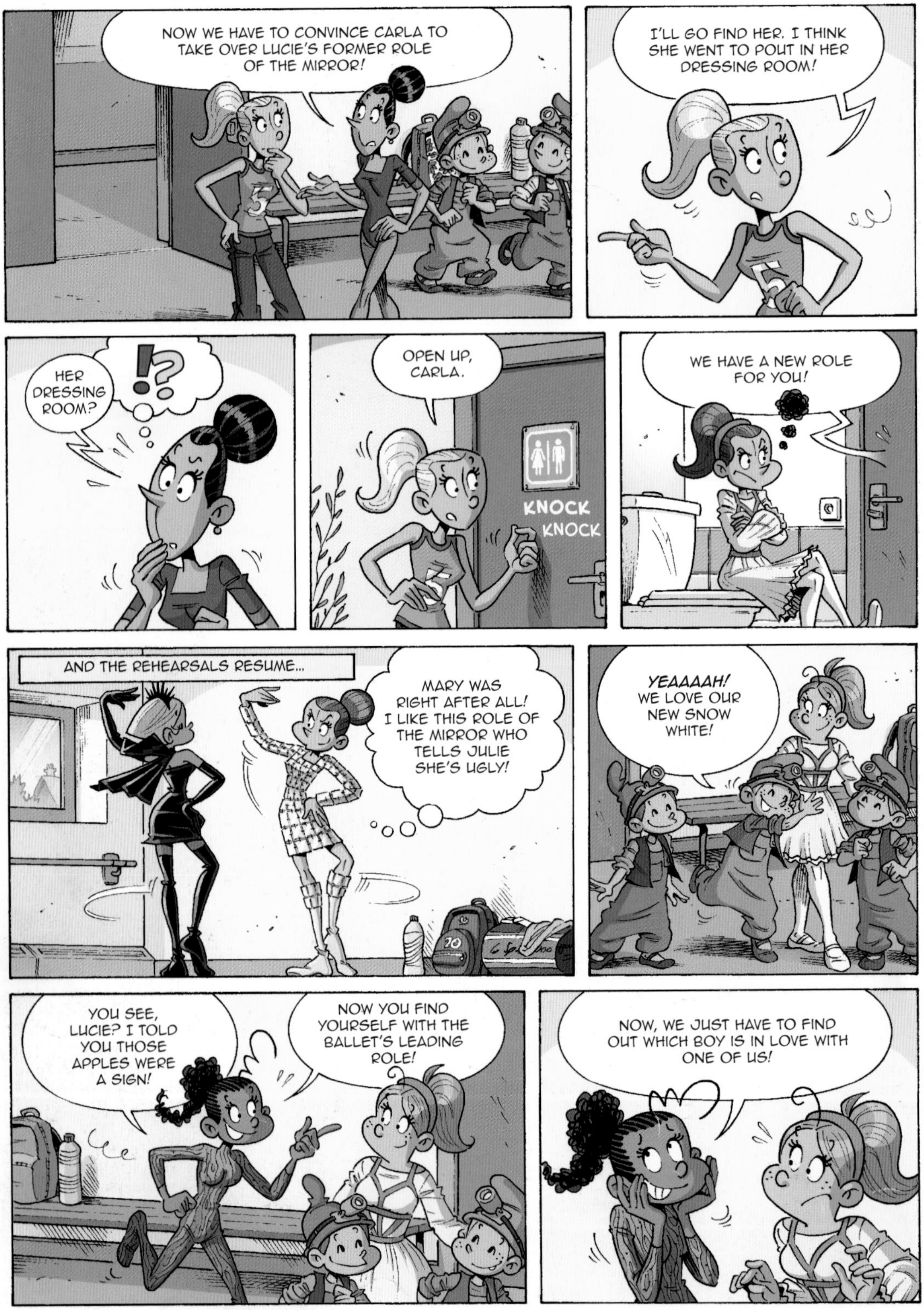
NOW WE HAVE TO CONVINCE CARLA TO TAKE OVER LUCIE'S FORMER ROLE OF THE MIRROR!
I'LL GO FIND HER. I THINK SHE WENT TO POUT IN HER DRESSING ROOM!
HER DRESSING ROOM?
!?
OPEN UP, CARLA.
KNOCK
KNOCK
WE HAVE A NEW ROLE FOR YOU!
AND THE REHEARSALS RESUME...
MARY WAS RIGHT AFTER ALL! I LIKE THIS ROLE OF THE MIRROR WHO TELLS JULIE SHE'S UGLY!
YEAAAAH! WE LOVE OUR NEW SNOW WHITE!
YOU SEE, LUCIE? I TOLD YOU THOSE APPLES WERE A SIGN!
NOW YOU FIND YOURSELF WITH THE BALLET'S LEADING ROLE!
NOW, WE JUST HAVE TO FIND OUT WHICH BOY IS IN LOVE WITH ONE OF US!

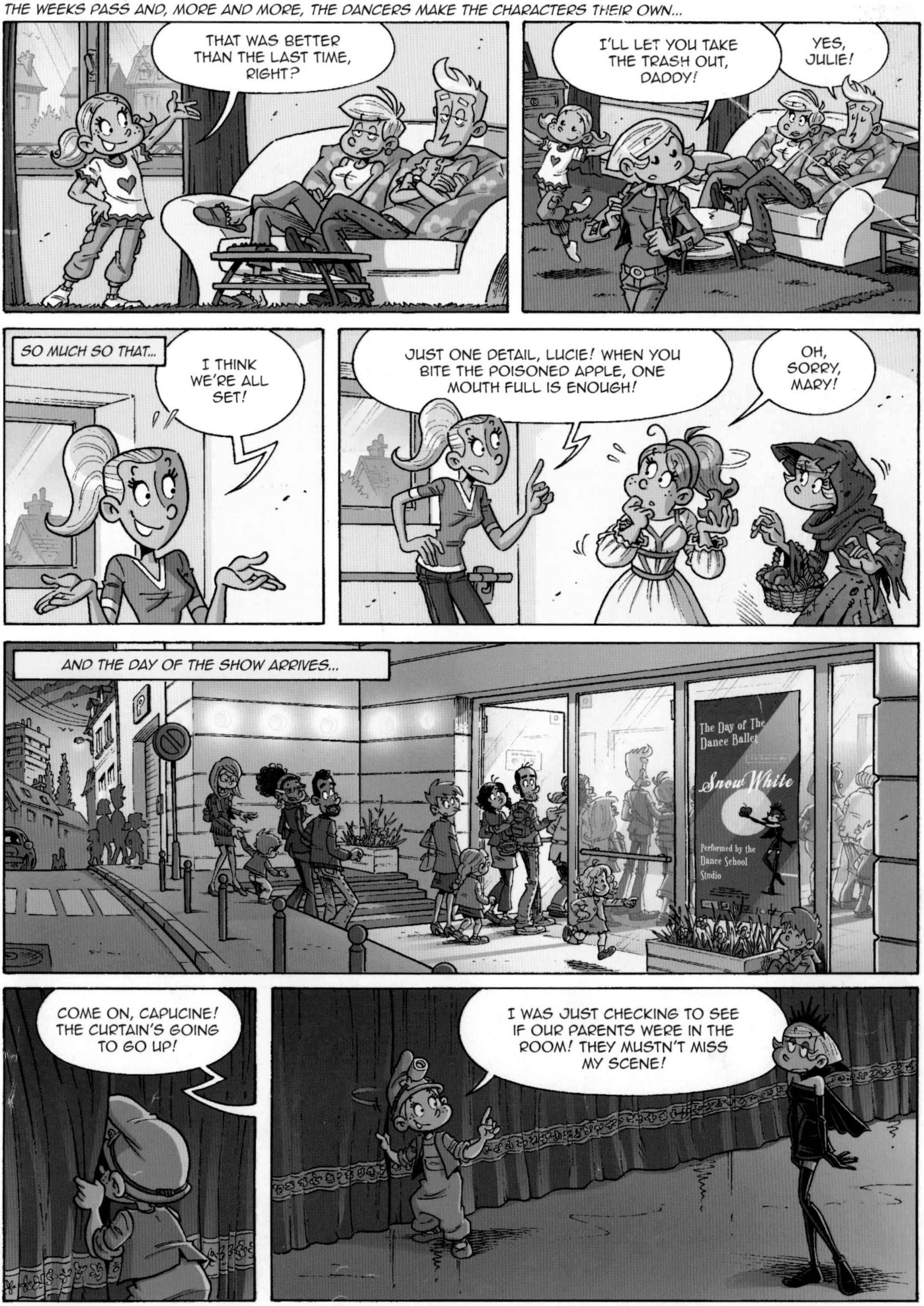
THE WEEKS PASS AND, MORE AND MORE, THE DANCERS MAKE THE CHARACTERS THEIR OWN...
THAT WAS BETTER THAN THE LAST TIME, RIGHT?
I'LL LET YOU TAKE THE TRASH OUT, DADDY!
YES, JULIE!
SO MUCH SO THAT...
I THINK WE'RE ALL SET!
JUST ONE DETAIL, LUCIE! WHEN YOU BITE THE POISONED APPLE, ONE MOUTH FULL IS ENOUGH!
OH, SORRY, MARY!
AND THE DAY OF THE SHOW ARRIVES...
The Day of The Dance Ballet
Snow White
Performed by the Dance School Studio
COME ON, CAPUCINE! THE CURTAIN'S GOING TO GO UP!
I WAS JUST CHECKING TO SEE IF OUR PARENTS WERE IN THE ROOM! THEY MUSTN'T MISS MY SCENE!

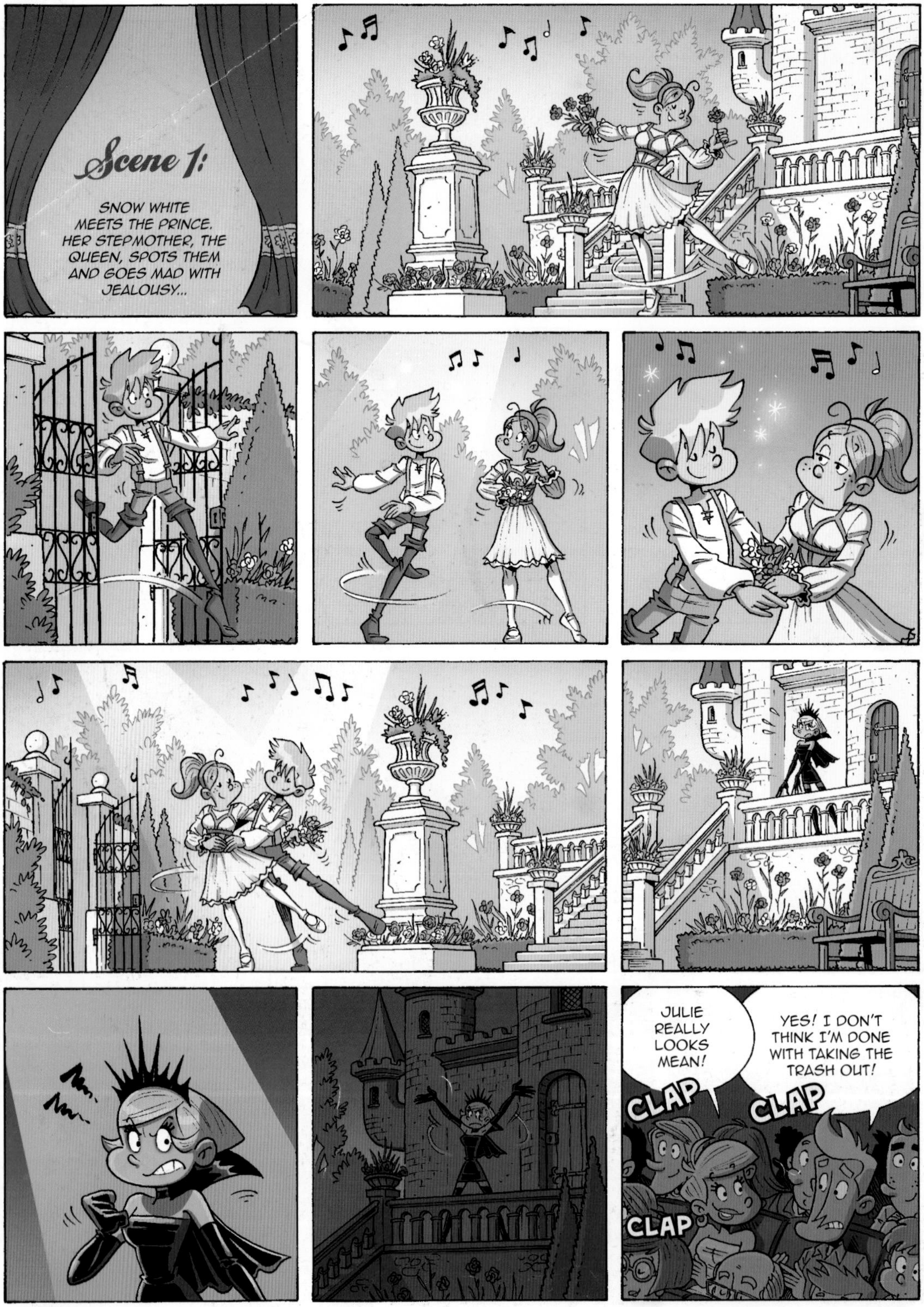
Scene 1:
SNOW WHITE MEETS THE PRINCE. HER STEPMOTHER, THE QUEEN, SPOTS THEM AND GOES MAD WITH JEALOUSY...
JULIE REALLY LOOKS MEAN!
YES! I DON'T THINK I'M DONE WITH TAKING THE TRASH OUT!
CLAP
CLAP
CLAP

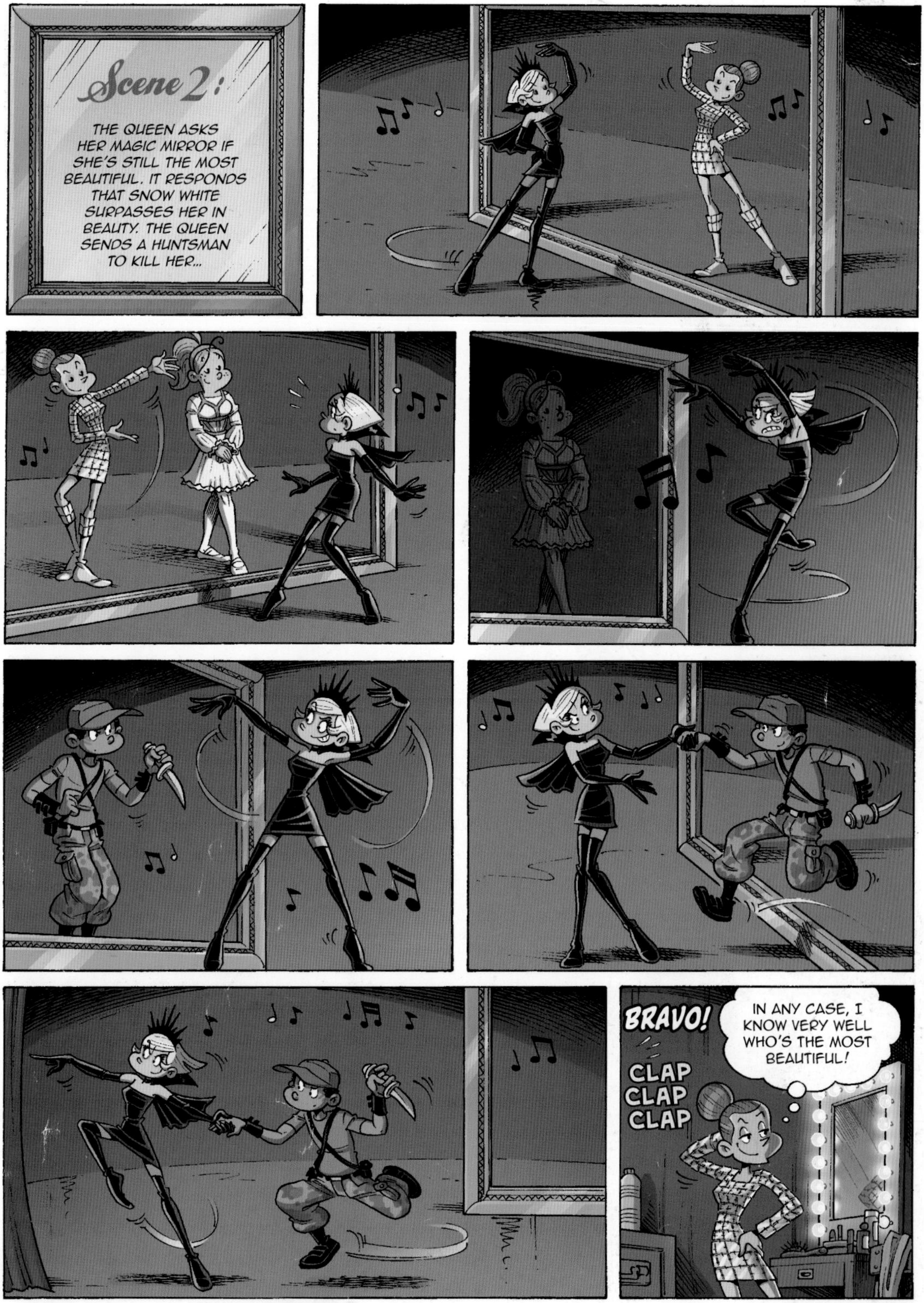
Scene 2:
THE QUEEN ASKS HER MAGIC MIRROR IF SHE'S STILL THE MOST BEAUTIFUL. IT RESPONDS THAT SNOW WHITE SURPASSES HER IN BEAUTY. THE QUEEN SENDS A HUNTSMAN TO KILL HER...
BRAVO!
CLAP CLAP CLAP
IN ANY CASE, I KNOW VERY WELL WHO'S THE MOST BEAUTIFUL!

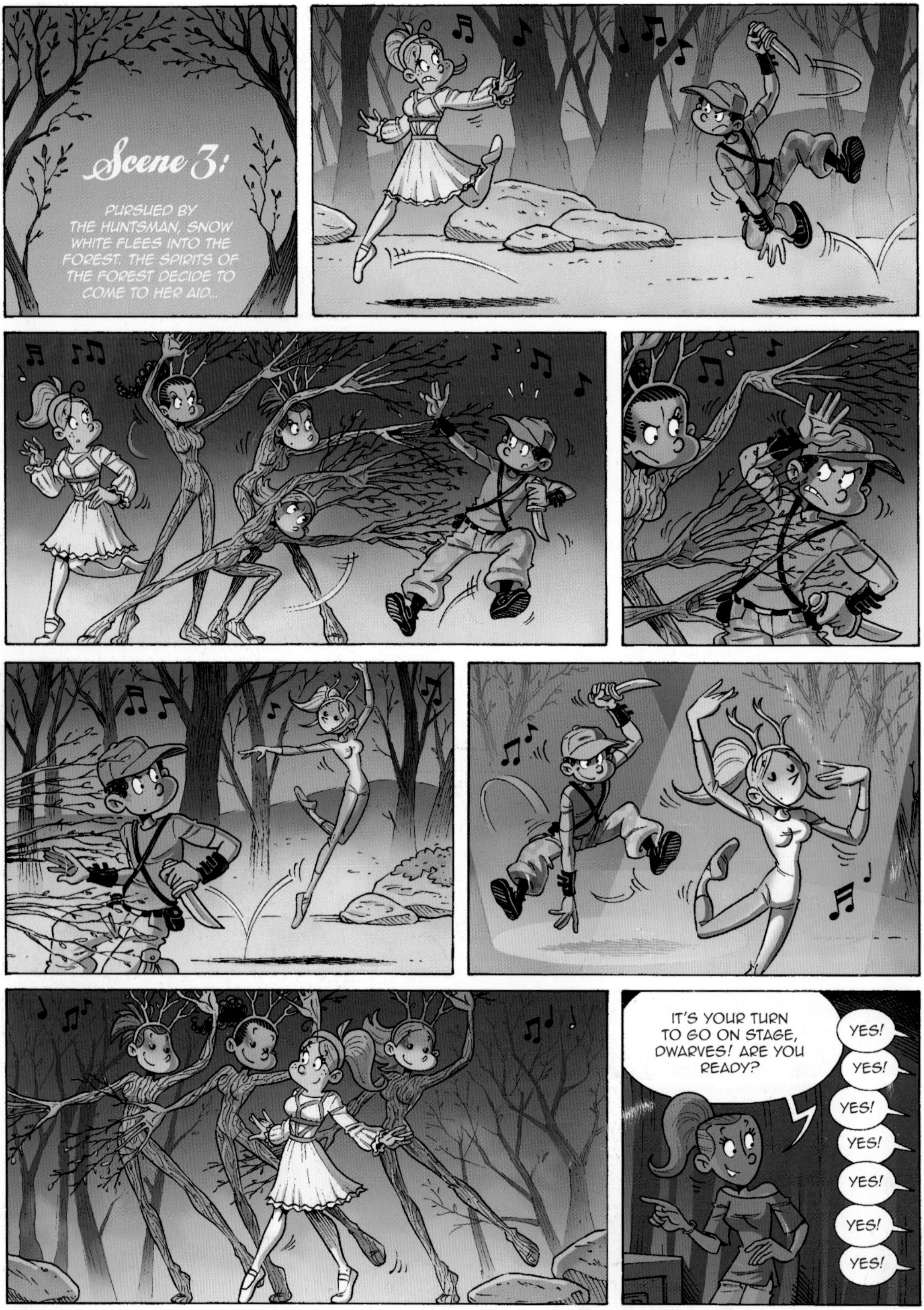
Scene 3:
PURSUED BY THE HUNTSMAN, SNOW WHITE FLEES INTO THE FOREST. THE SPIRITS OF THE FOREST DECIDE TO COME TO HER AID...
IT'S YOUR TURN TO GO ON STAGE, DWARVES! ARE YOU READY?
YES!
YES!
YES!
YES!
YES!
YES!
YES!

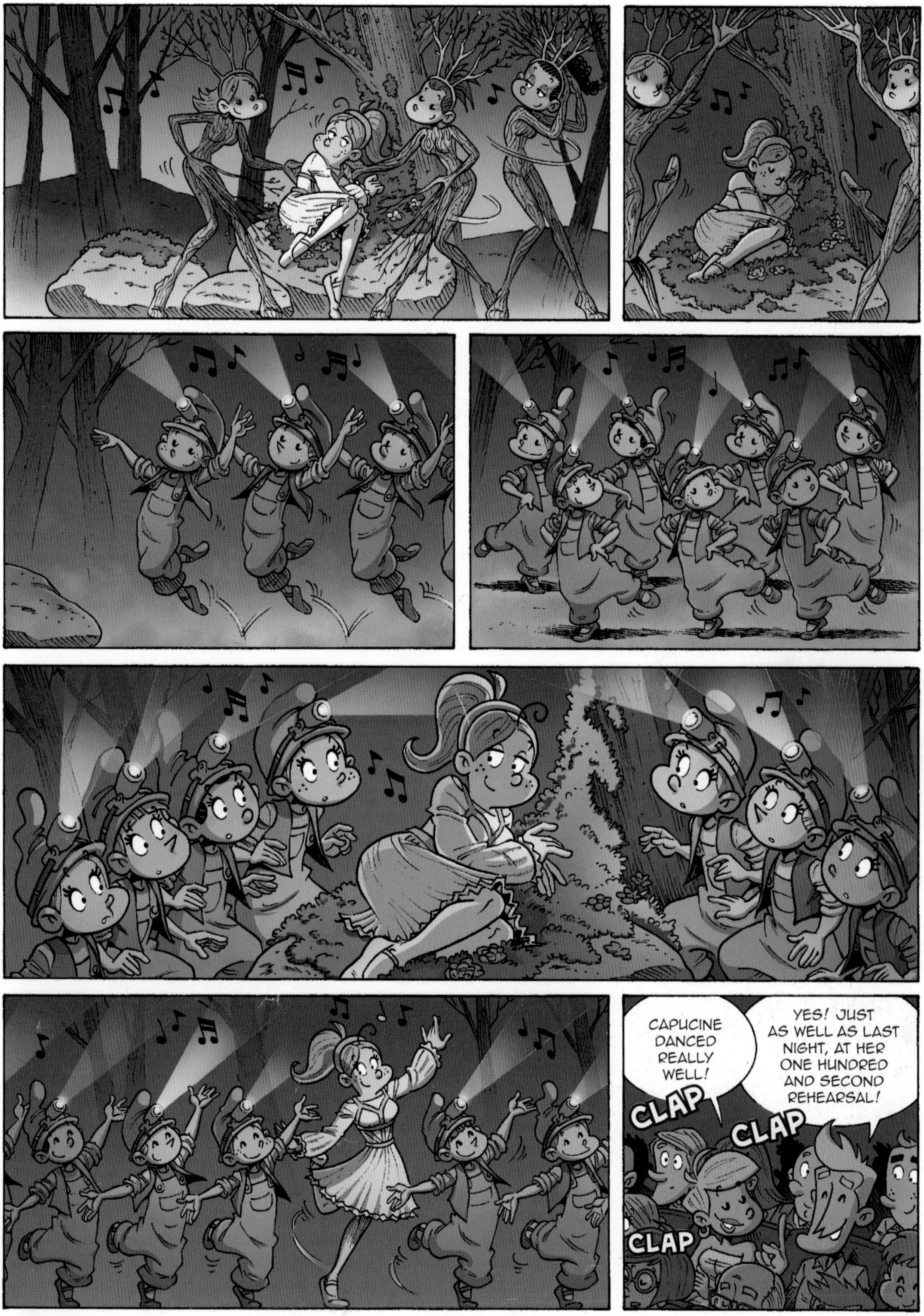
CAPUCINE DANCED REALLY WELL!
CLAP
YES! JUST AS WELL AS LAST NIGHT, AT HER ONE HUNDRED AND SECOND REHEARSAL!
CLAP
CLAP

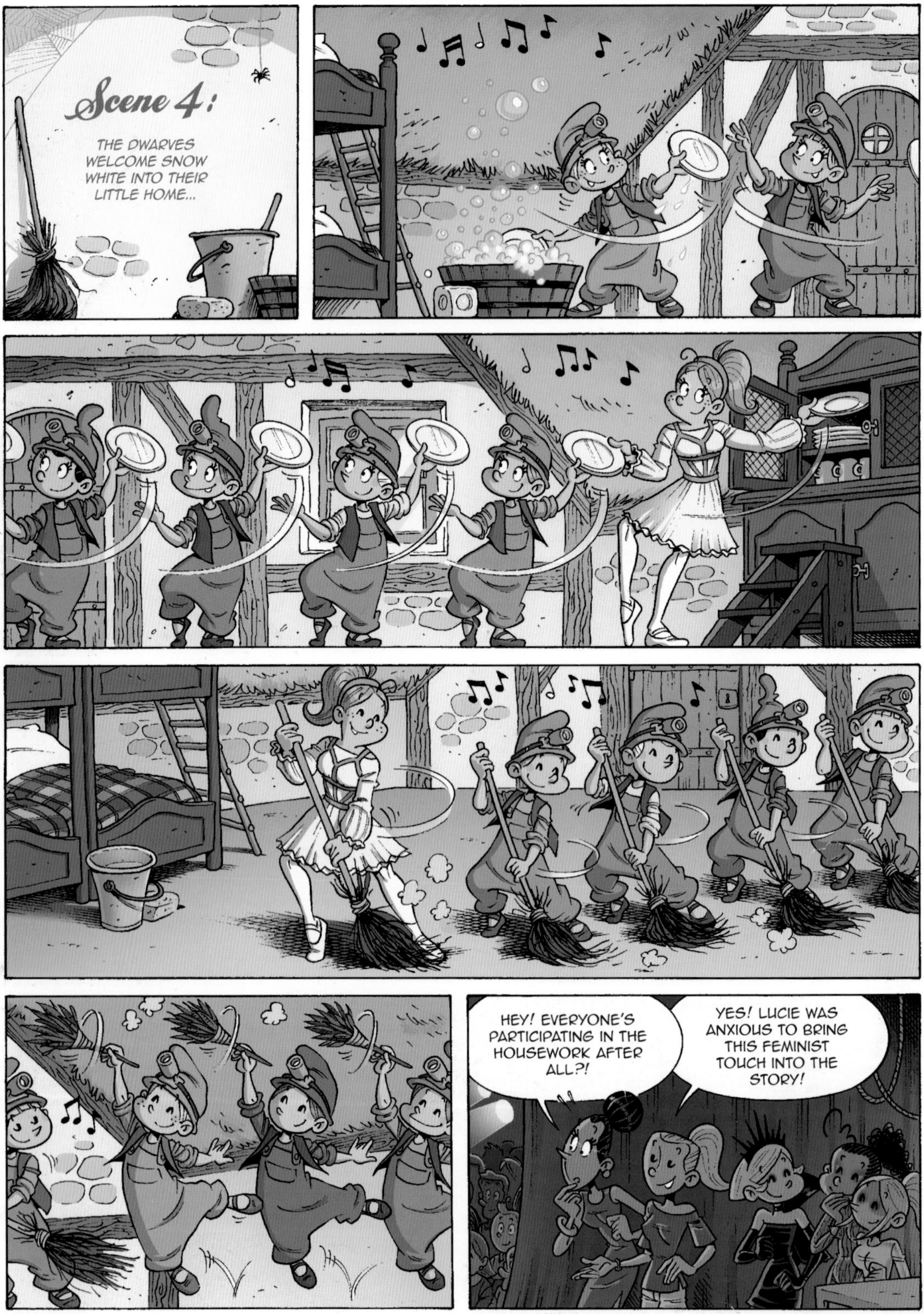
Scene 4:
THE DWARVES WELCOME SNOW WHITE INTO THEIR LITTLE HOME...
HEY! EVERYONE'S PARTICIPATING IN THE HOUSEWORK AFTER ALL?!
YES! LUCIE WAS ANXIOUS TO BRING THIS FEMINIST TOUCH INTO THE STORY!

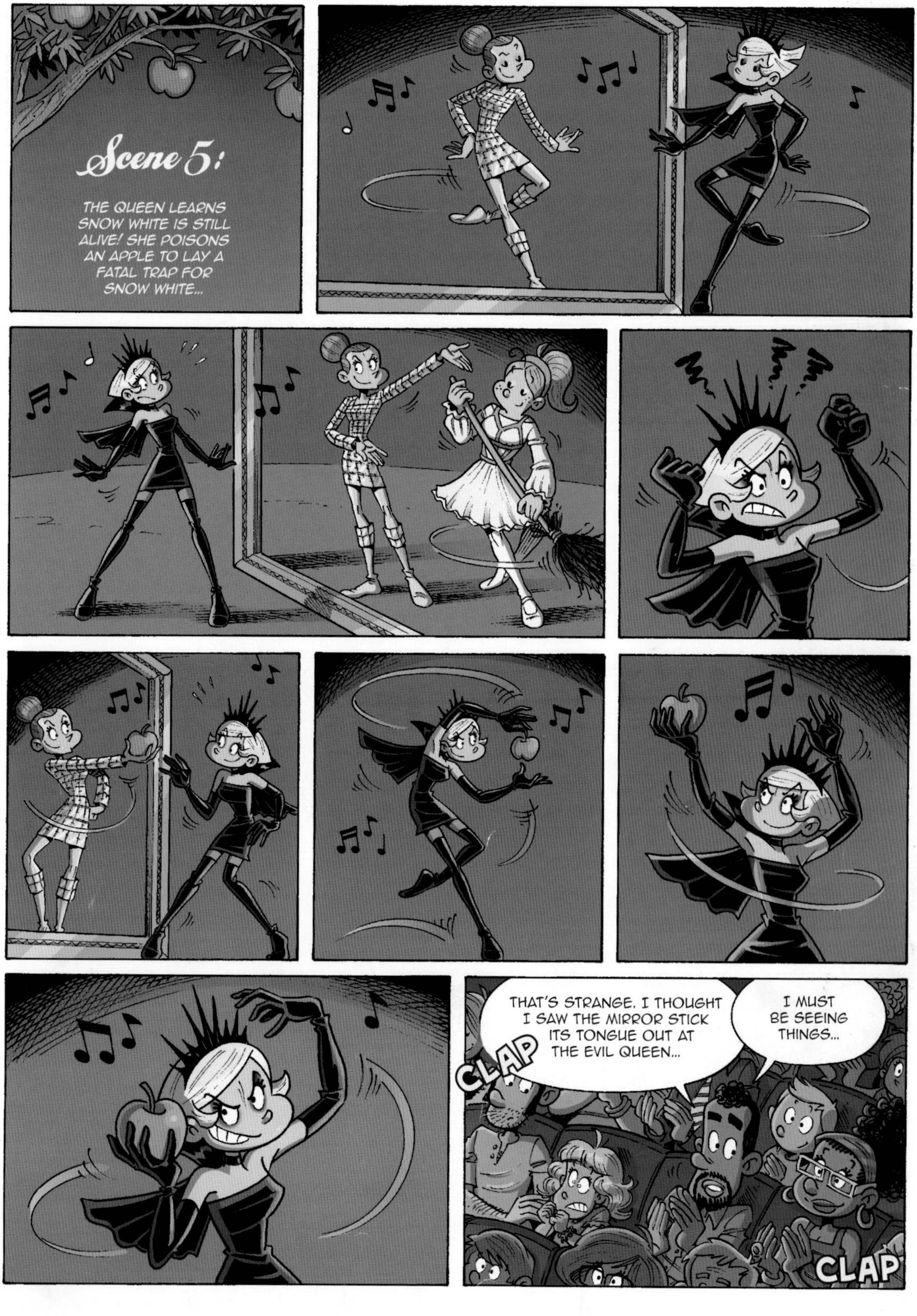
Scene 5:
THE QUEEN LEARNS SNOW WHITE IS STILL ALIVE! SHE POISONS AN APPLE TO LAY A FATAL TRAP FOR SNOW WHITE...
CLAP
THAT'S STRANGE. I THOUGHT I SAW THE MIRROR STICK ITS TONGUE OUT AT THE EVIL QUEEN...
I MUST BE SEEING THINGS...
CLAP

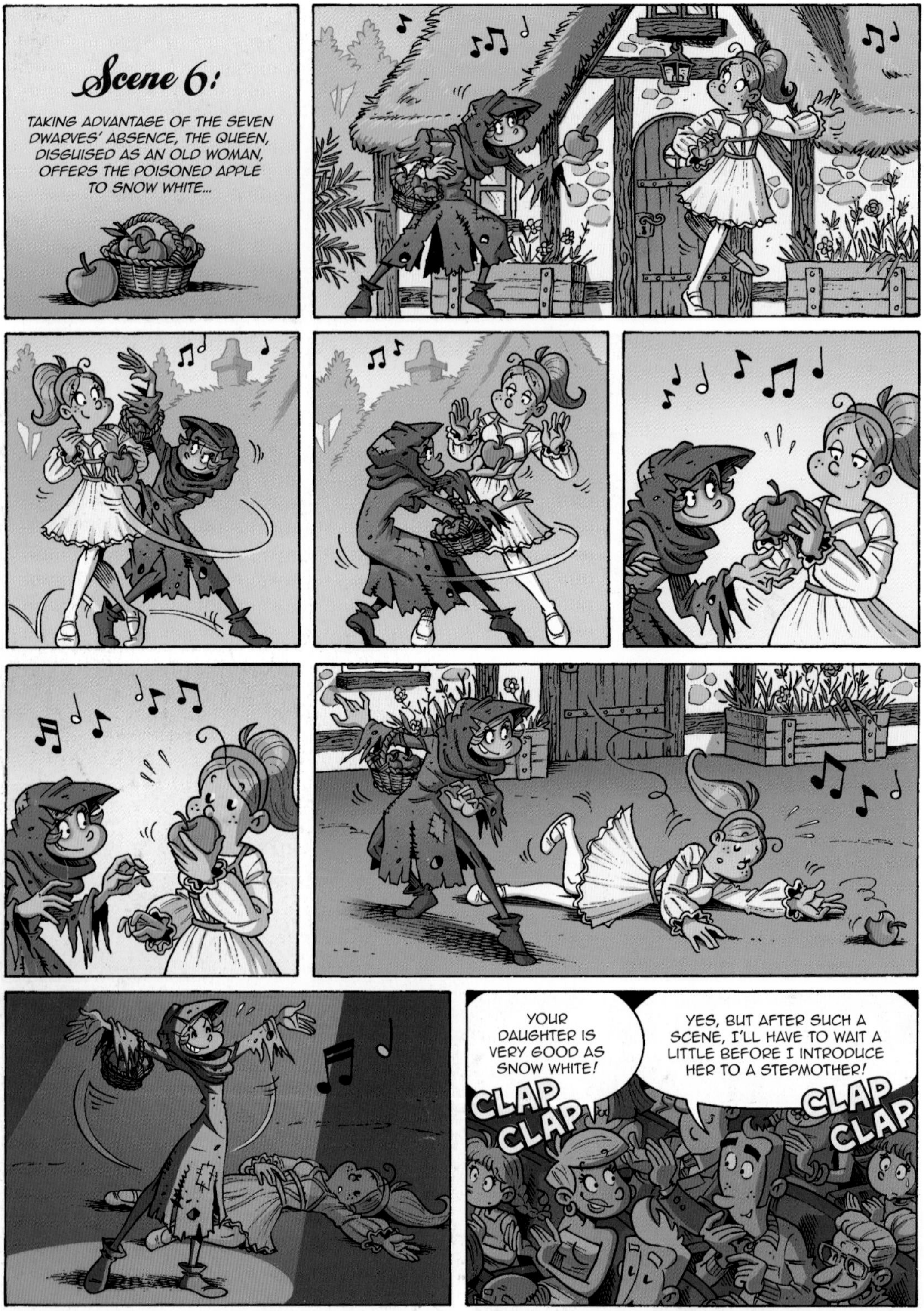
Scene 6:
TAKING ADVANTAGE OF THE SEVEN DWARVES' ABSENCE, THE QUEEN, DISGUISED AS AN OLD WOMAN, OFFERS THE POISONED APPLE TO SNOW WHITE...
YOUR DAUGHTER IS VERY GOOD AS SNOW WHITE!
YES, BUT AFTER SUCH A SCENE, I'LL HAVE TO WAIT A LITTLE BEFORE I INTRODUCE HER TO A STEPMOTHER!
CLAP CLAP
CLAP CLAP

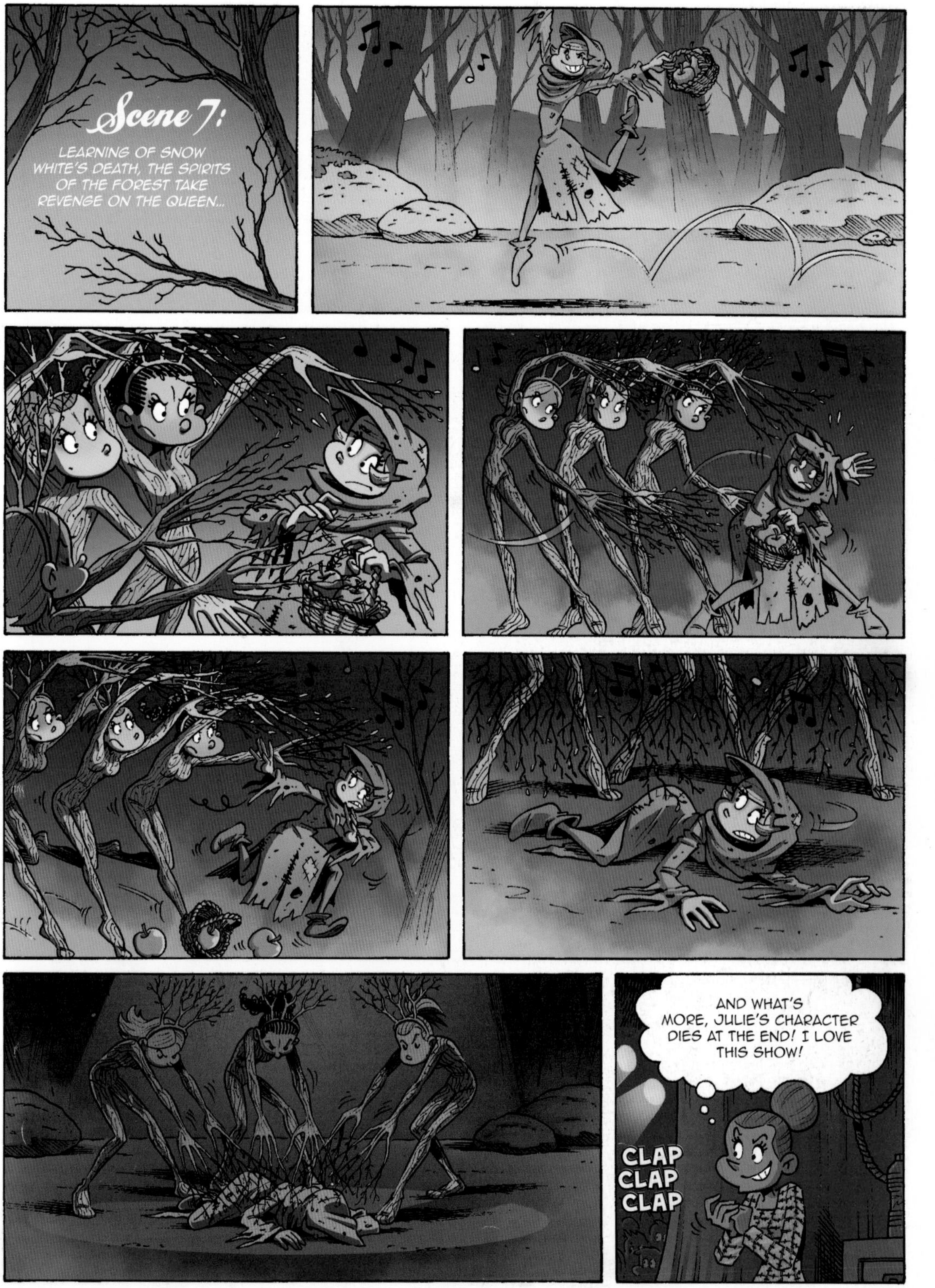
Scene 7:
LEARNING OF SNOW WHITE'S DEATH, THE SPIRITS OF THE FOREST TAKE REVENGE ON THE QUEEN...
AND WHAT'S MORE, JULIE'S CHARACTER DIES AT THE END! I LOVE THIS SHOW!
CLAP
CLAP
CLAP

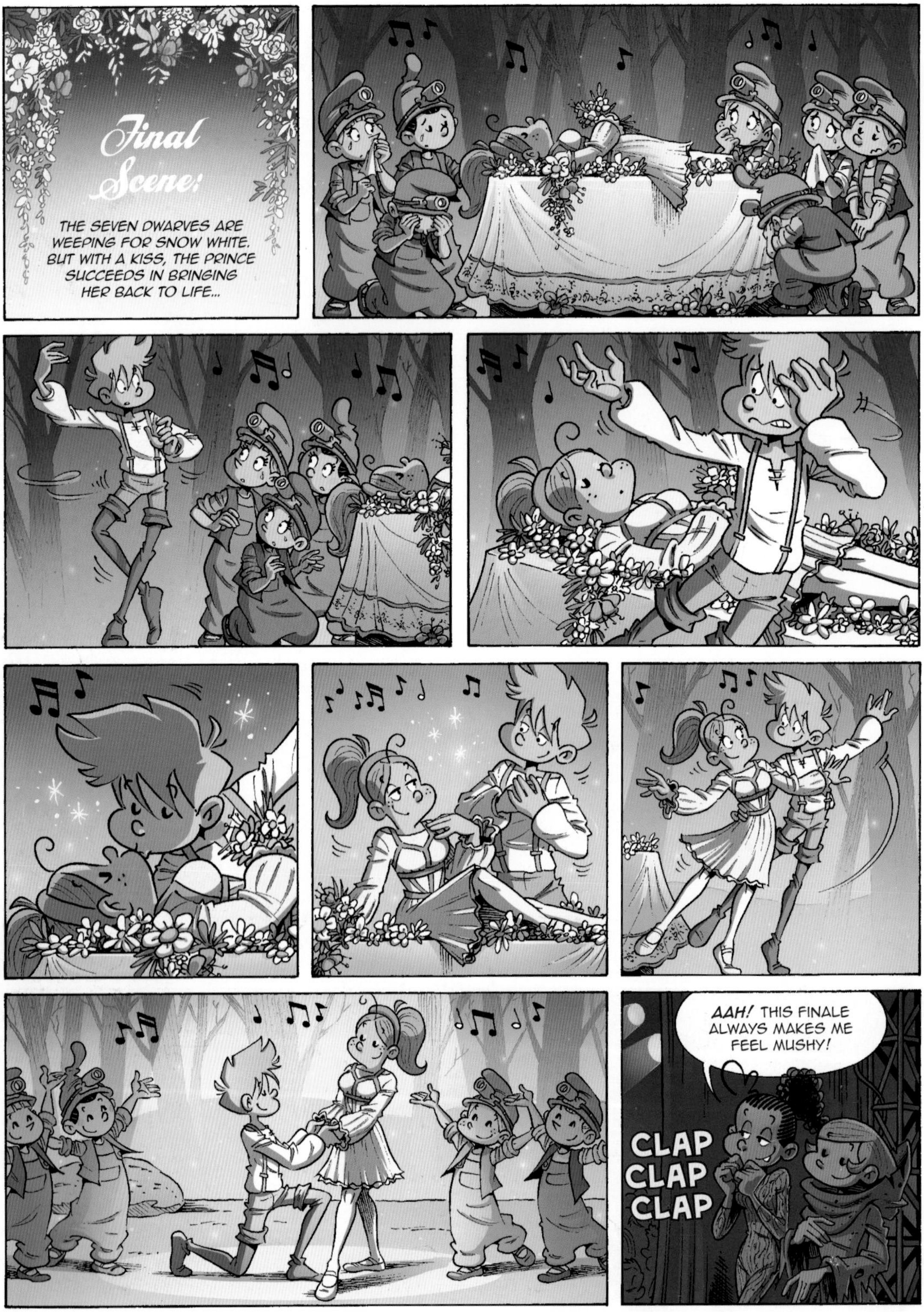
Final Scene:
THE SEVEN DWARVES ARE WEEPING FOR SNOW WHITE. BUT WITH A KISS, THE PRINCE SUCCEEDS IN BRINGING HER BACK TO LIFE...
AAH! THIS FINALE ALWAYS MAKES ME FEEL MUSHY!
CLAP
CLAP
CLAP

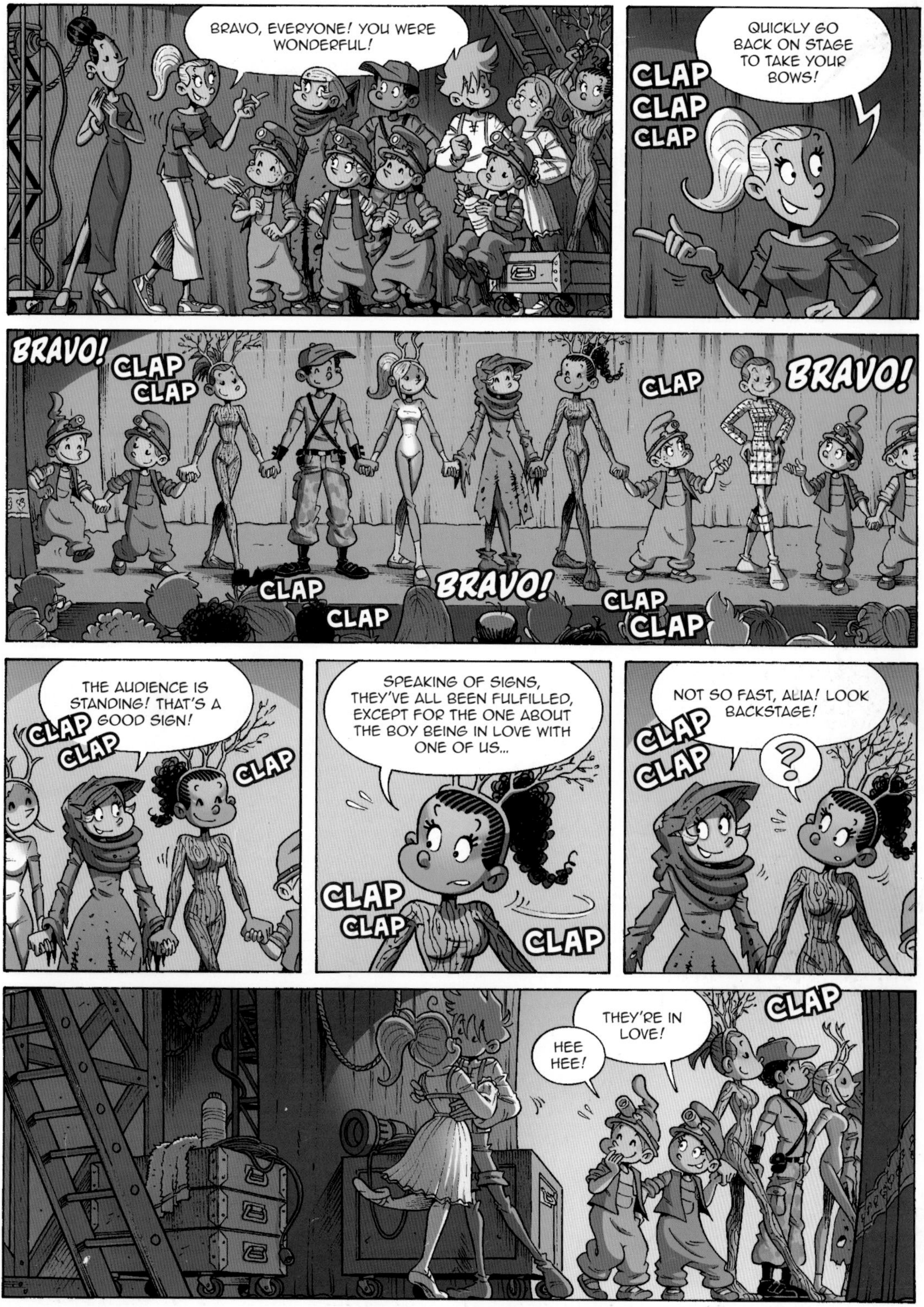

BRAVO, EVERYONE! YOU WERE WONDERFUL!
CLAP CLAP CLAP
QUICKLY GO BACK ON STAGE TO TAKE YOUR BOWS!
BRAVO!
CLAP CLAP
CLAP
BRAVO!
CLAP
CLAP
BRAVO!
CLAP CLAP
CLAP CLAP
THE AUDIENCE IS STANDING! THAT'S A GOOD SIGN!
CLAP
SPEAKING OF SIGNS, THEY'VE ALL BEEN FULFILLED, EXCEPT FOR THE ONE ABOUT THE BOY BEING IN LOVE WITH ONE OF US...
CLAP CLAP
CLAP
CLAP CLAP
NOT SO FAST, ALIA! LOOK BACKSTAGE!
?
CLAP
THEY'RE IN LOVE!
HEE HEE!

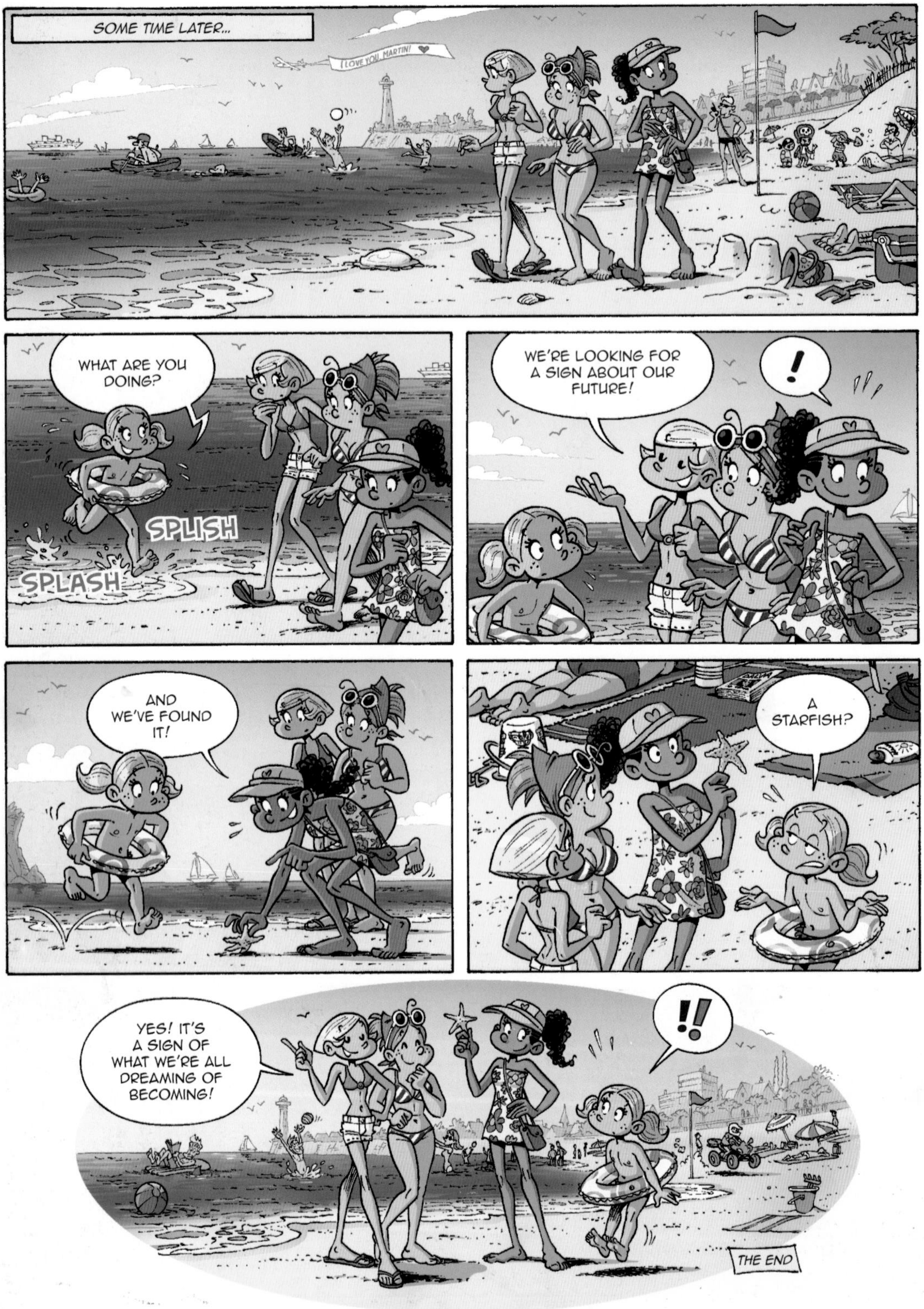
SOME TIME LATER...
I LOVE YOU, MARTIN!
WHAT ARE YOU DOING?
SPLISH
SPLASH
WE'RE LOOKING FOR A SIGN ABOUT OUR FUTURE!
!
AND WE'VE FOUND IT!
A STARFISH?
YES! IT'S A SIGN OF WHAT WE'RE ALL DREAMING OF BECOMING!
!!
THE END

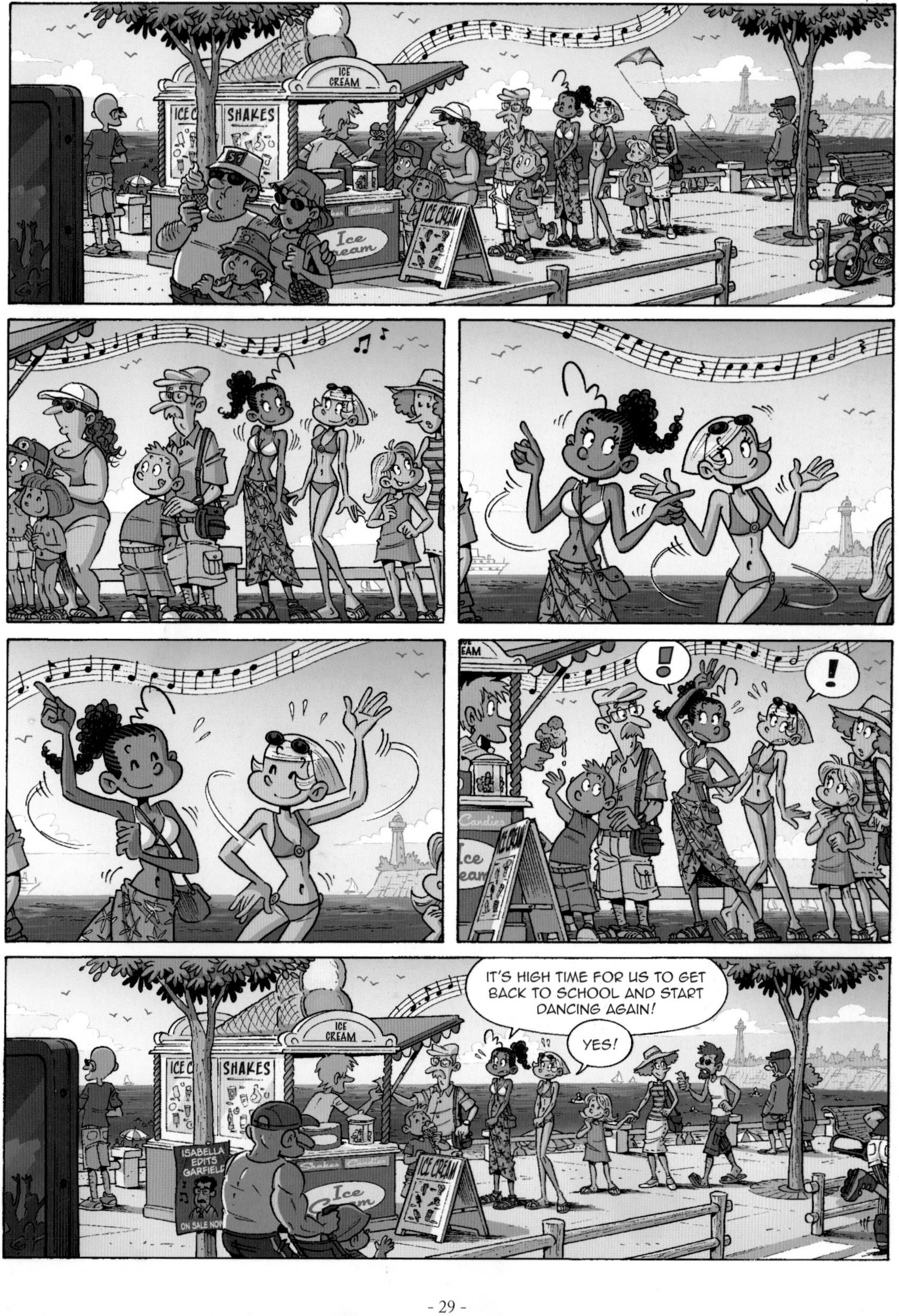
ICE CREAM
SHAKES
ICE CREAM
Candies
Ice Cream
!
!
IT'S HIGH TIME FOR US TO GET BACK TO SCHOOL AND START DANCING AGAIN!
YES!
ISABELLA EDITS GARFIELD
ON SALE NOW

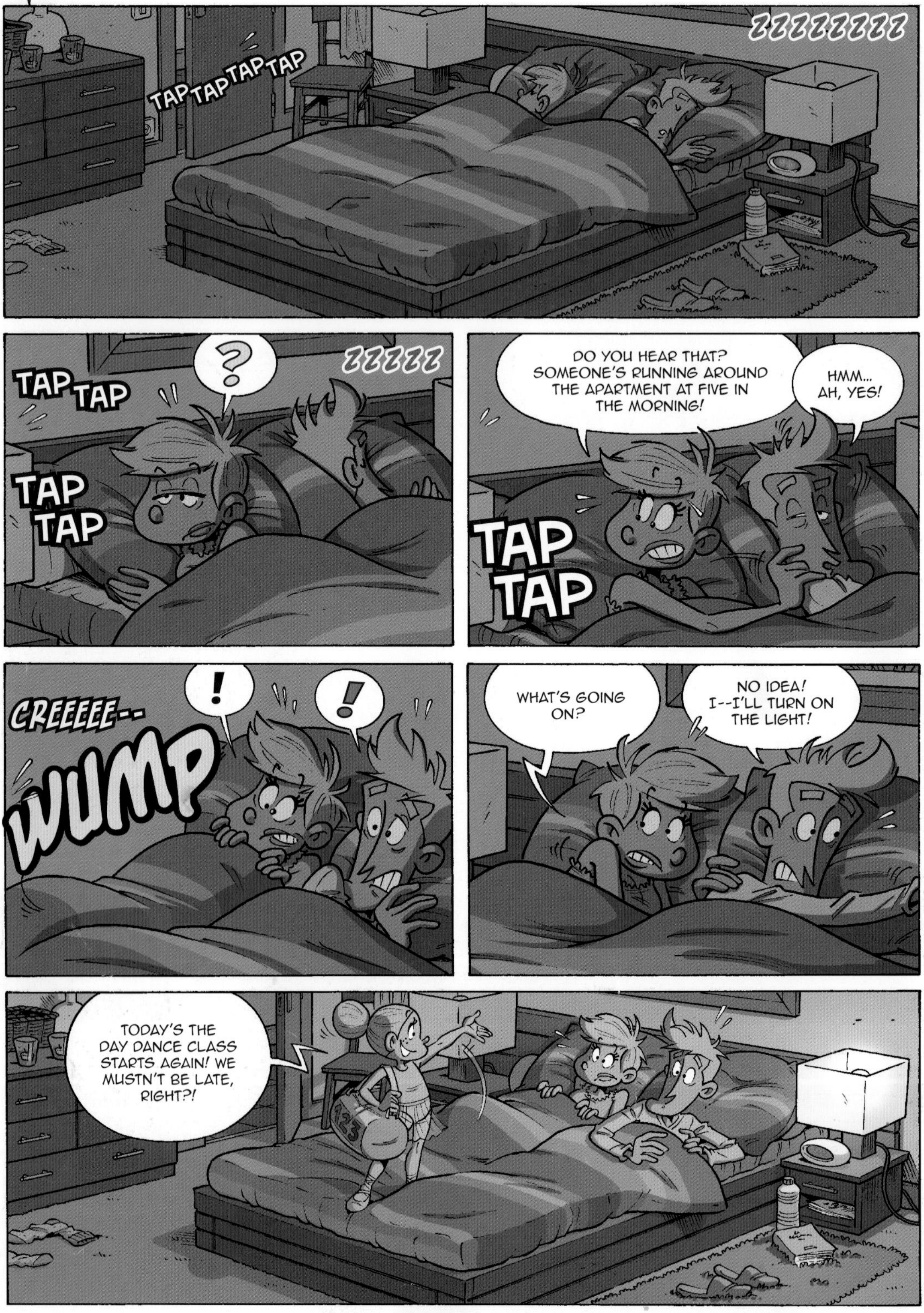
TAP TAP TAP TAP
ZZZZZZZZ
TAP TAP
?
ZZZZZ
TAP TAP
DO YOU HEAR THAT? SOMEONE'S RUNNING AROUND THE APARTMENT AT FIVE IN THE MORNING!
HMM... AH, YES!
TAP TAP
CREEEEE--
WUMP
!
!
WHAT'S GOING ON?
NO IDEA! I--I'LL TURN ON THE LIGHT!
TODAY'S THE DAY DANCE CLASS STARTS AGAIN! WE MUSTN'T BE LATE, RIGHT?!
123

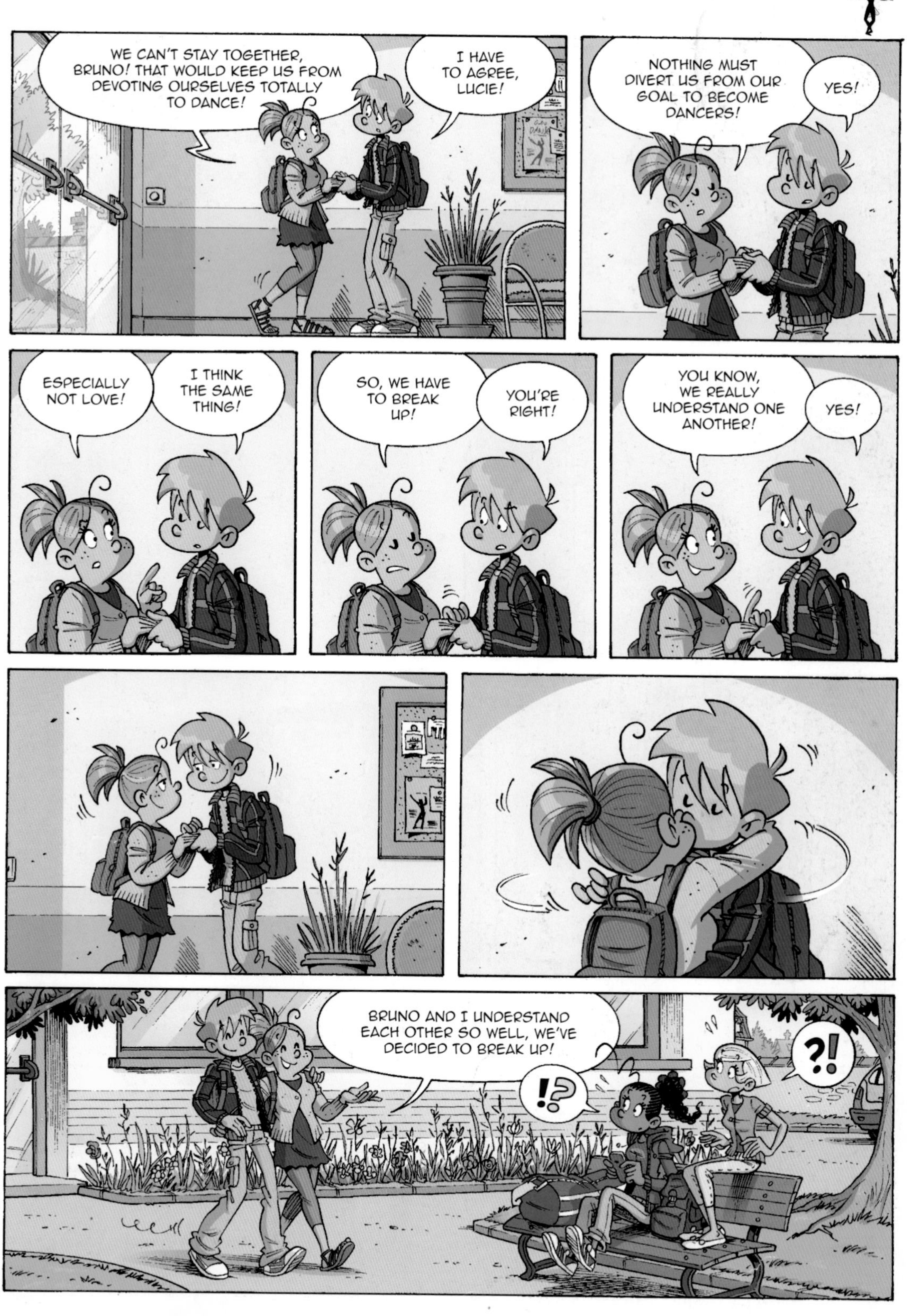
WE CAN'T STAY TOGETHER, BRUNO! THAT WOULD KEEP US FROM DEVOTING OURSELVES TOTALLY TO DANCE!
I HAVE TO AGREE, LUCIE!
NOTHING MUST DIVERT US FROM OUR GOAL TO BECOME DANCERS!
YES!
ESPECIALLY NOT LOVE!
I THINK THE SAME THING!
SO, WE HAVE TO BREAK UP!
YOU'RE RIGHT!
YOU KNOW, WE REALLY UNDERSTAND ONE ANOTHER!
YES!
BRUNO AND I UNDERSTAND EACH OTHER SO WELL, WE'VE DECIDED TO BREAK UP!
!?
?!

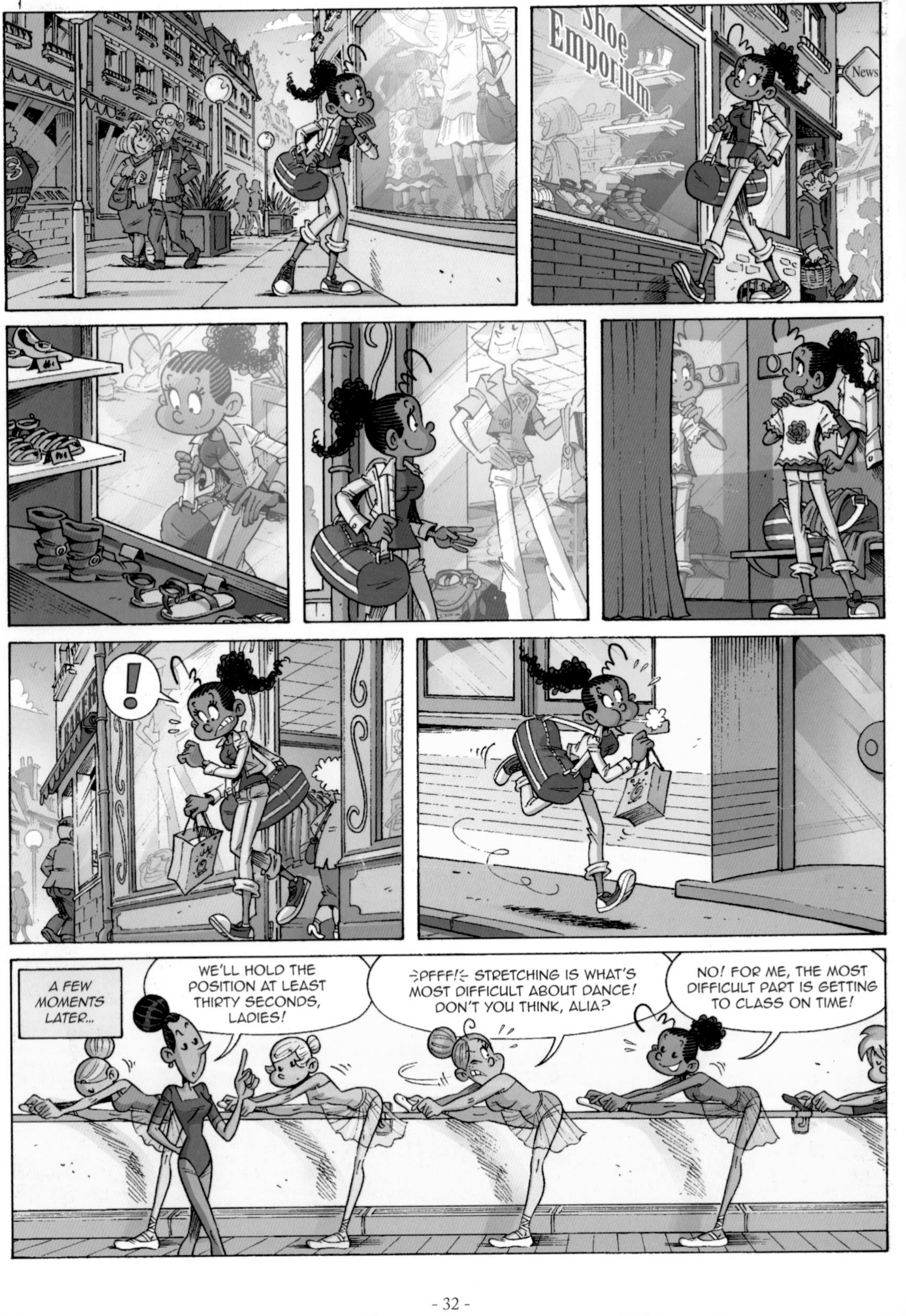
Shoe Emporium
News
!
A FEW MOMENTS LATER...
WE'LL HOLD THE POSITION AT LEAST THIRTY SECONDS, LADIES!
PFFF! STRETCHING IS WHAT'S MOST DIFFICULT ABOUT DANCE! DON'T YOU THINK, ALIA?
NO! FOR ME, THE MOST DIFFICULT PART IS GETTING TO CLASS ON TIME!

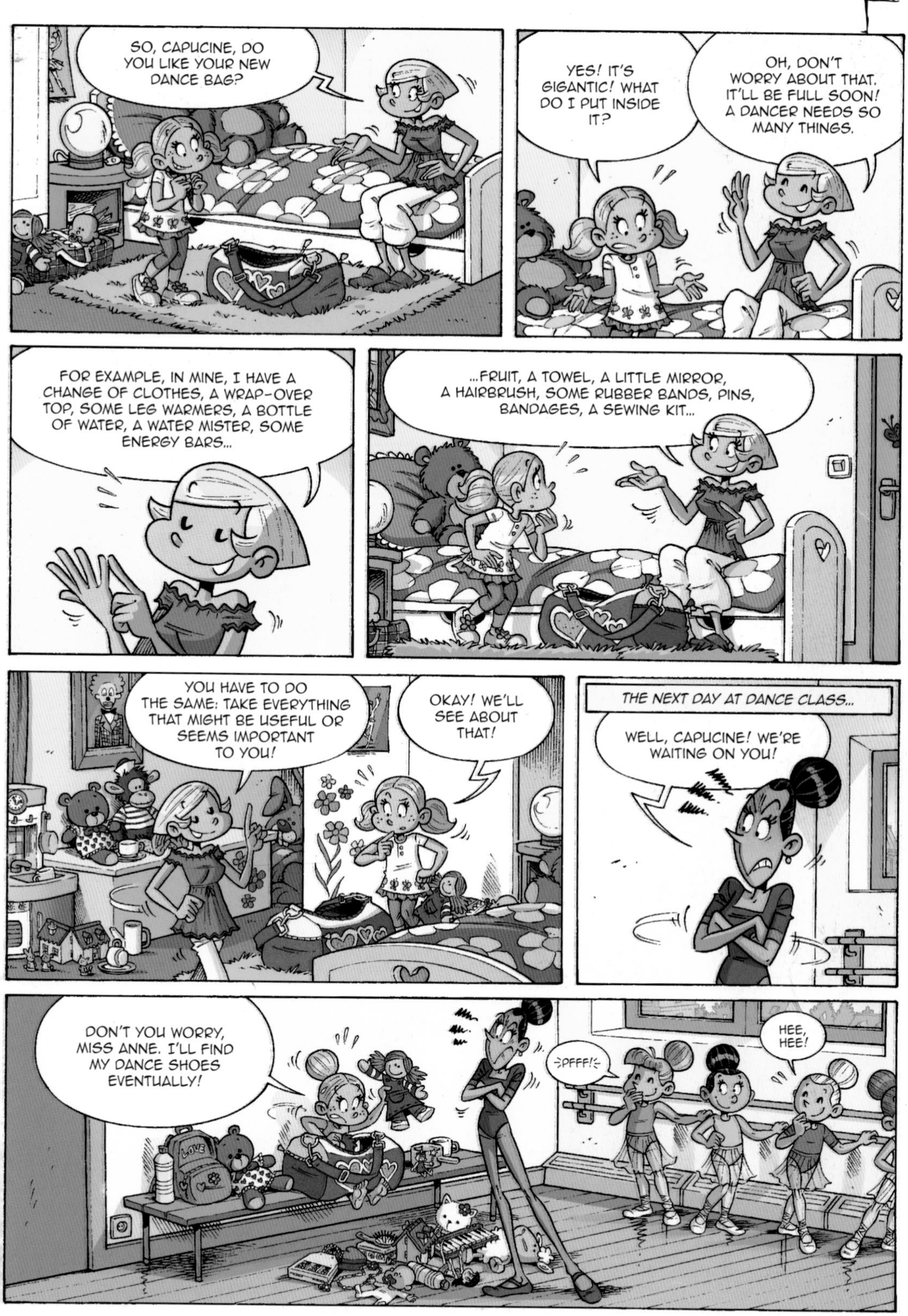
SO, CAPUCINE, DO YOU LIKE YOUR NEW DANCE BAG?
YES! IT'S GIGANTIC! WHAT DO I PUT INSIDE IT?
OH, DON'T WORRY ABOUT THAT. IT'LL BE FULL SOON! A DANCER NEEDS SO MANY THINGS.
FOR EXAMPLE, IN MINE, I HAVE A CHANGE OF CLOTHES, A WRAP-OVER TOP, SOME LEG WARMERS, A BOTTLE OF WATER, A WATER MISTER, SOME ENERGY BARS...
...FRUIT, A TOWEL, A LITTLE MIRROR, A HAIRBRUSH, SOME RUBBER BANDS, PINS, BANDAGES, A SEWING KIT...
YOU HAVE TO DO THE SAME: TAKE EVERYTHING THAT MIGHT BE USEFUL OR SEEMS IMPORTANT TO YOU!
OKAY! WE'LL SEE ABOUT THAT!
THE NEXT DAY AT DANCE CLASS...
WELL, CAPUCINE! WE'RE WAITING ON YOU!
DON'T YOU WORRY, MISS ANNE. I'LL FIND MY DANCE SHOES EVENTUALLY!
PFFF!
HEE, HEE!
LOVE

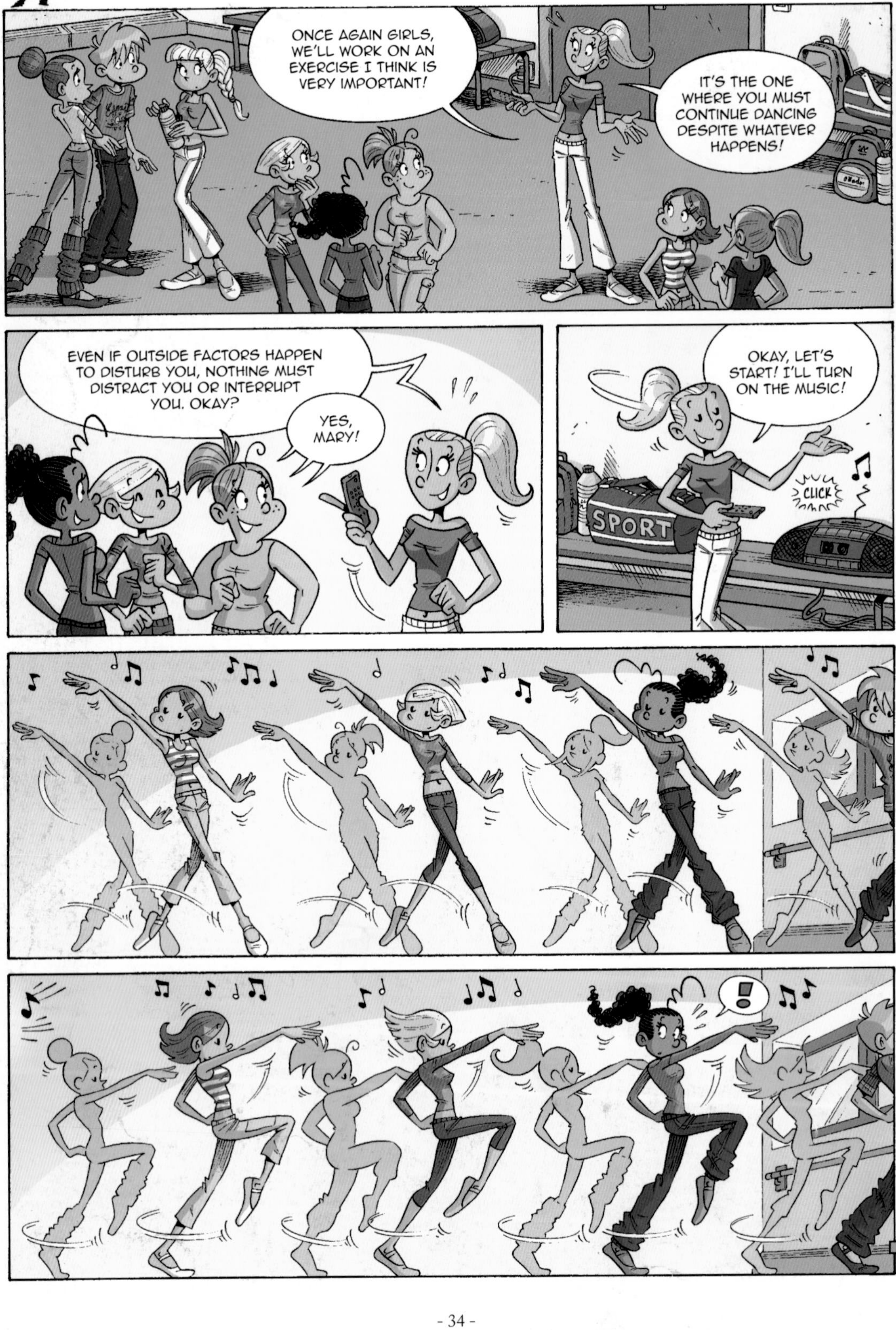
ONCE AGAIN GIRLS, WE'LL WORK ON AN EXERCISE I THINK IS VERY IMPORTANT!
IT'S THE ONE WHERE YOU MUST CONTINUE DANCING DESPITE WHATEVER HAPPENS!
EVEN IF OUTSIDE FACTORS HAPPEN TO DISTURB YOU, NOTHING MUST DISTRACT YOU OR INTERRUPT YOU. OKAY?
YES, MARY!
OKAY, LET'S START! I'LL TURN ON THE MUSIC!
SPORT
CLICK
!

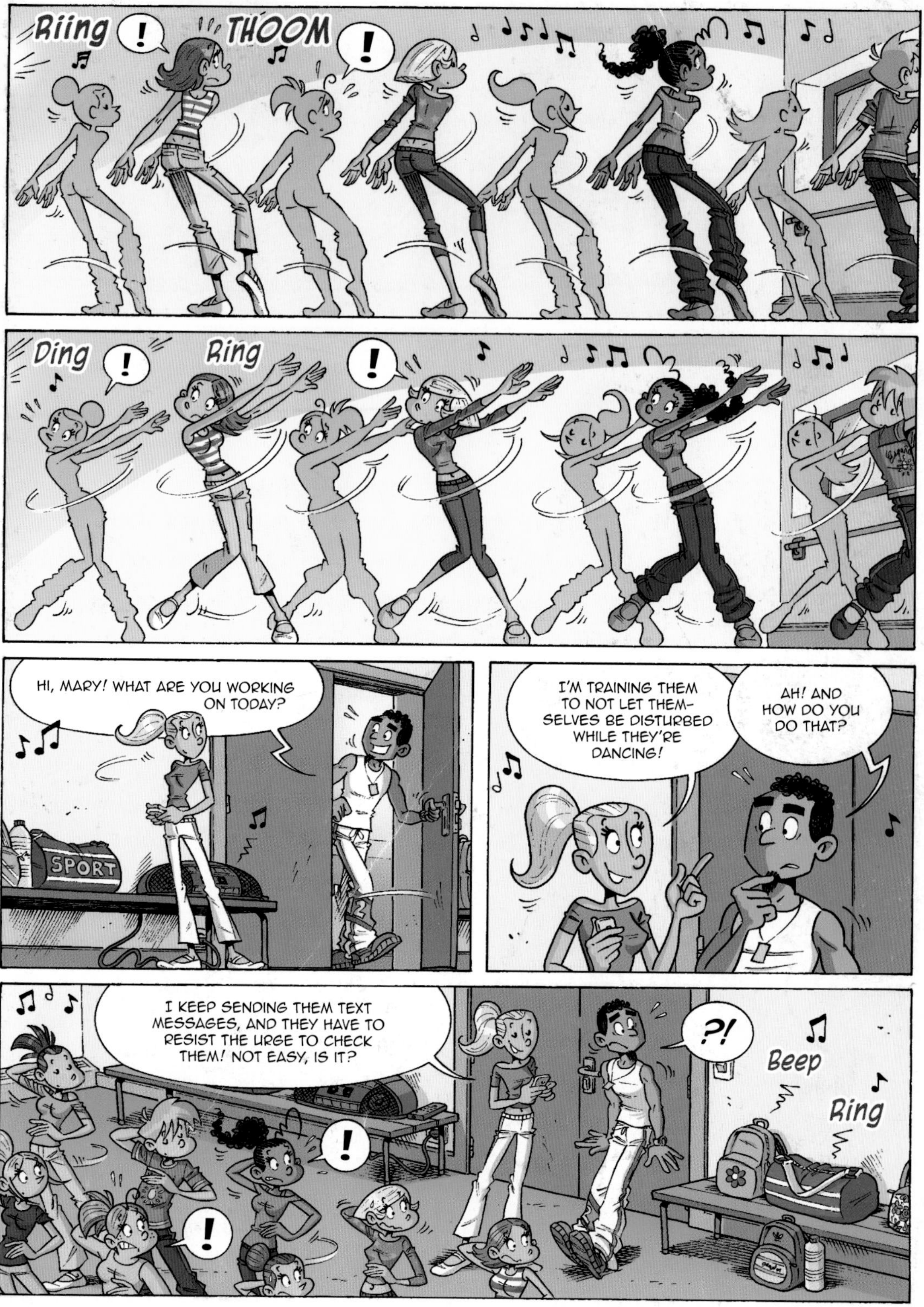
Riiing
!
THOOM
!
Ding
!
Ring
!
HI, MARY! WHAT ARE YOU WORKING ON TODAY?
SPORT
I'M TRAINING THEM TO NOT LET THEM-SELVES BE DISTURBED WHILE THEY'RE DANCING!
AH! AND HOW DO YOU DO THAT?
I KEEP SENDING THEM TEXT MESSAGES, AND THEY HAVE TO RESIST THE URGE TO CHECK THEM! NOT EASY, IS IT?
?!
Beep
Ring
!
!

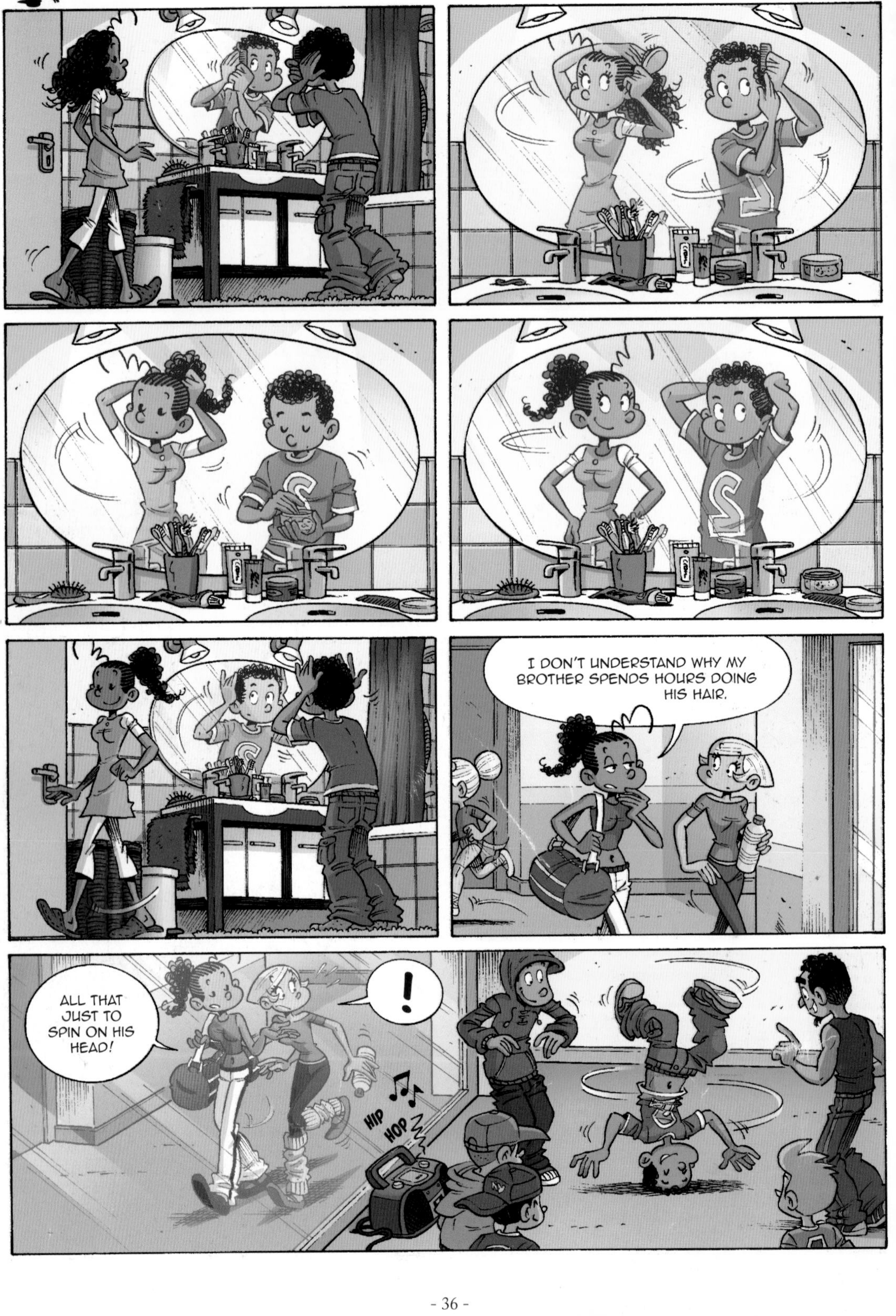
I DON'T UNDERSTAND WHY MY BROTHER SPENDS HOURS DOING HIS HAIR.
ALL THAT JUST TO SPIN ON HIS HEAD!
!
HIP HOP

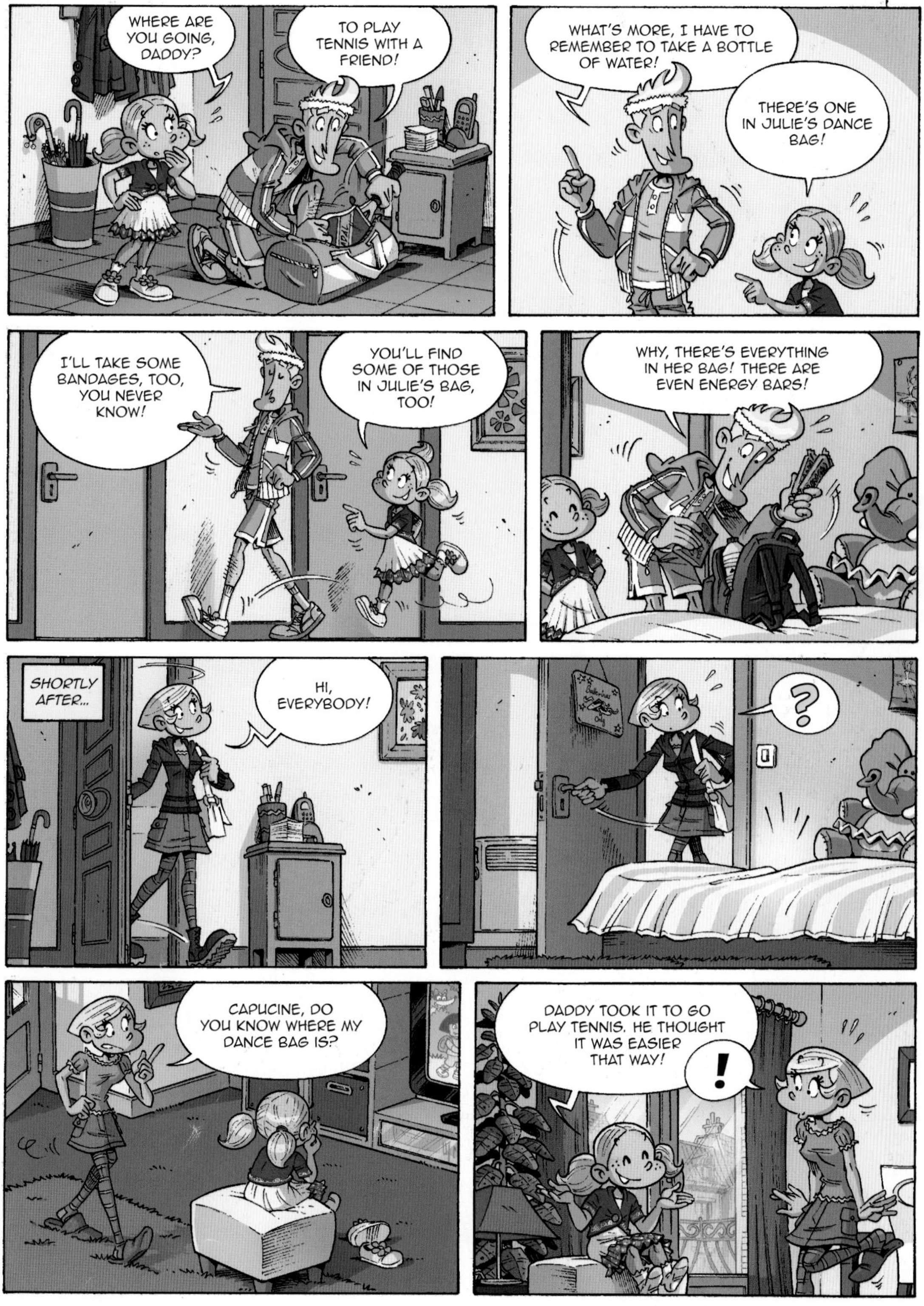
WHERE ARE YOU GOING, DADDY?
TO PLAY TENNIS WITH A FRIEND!
WHAT'S MORE, I HAVE TO REMEMBER TO TAKE A BOTTLE OF WATER!
THERE'S ONE IN JULIE'S DANCE BAG!
I'LL TAKE SOME BANDAGES, TOO, YOU NEVER KNOW!
YOU'LL FIND SOME OF THOSE IN JULIE'S BAG, TOO!
WHY, THERE'S EVERYTHING IN HER BAG! THERE ARE EVEN ENERGY BARS!
SHORTLY AFTER...
HI, EVERYBODY!
?
CAPUCINE, DO YOU KNOW WHERE MY DANCE BAG IS?
DADDY TOOK IT TO GO PLAY TENNIS. HE THOUGHT IT WAS EASIER THAT WAY!
!

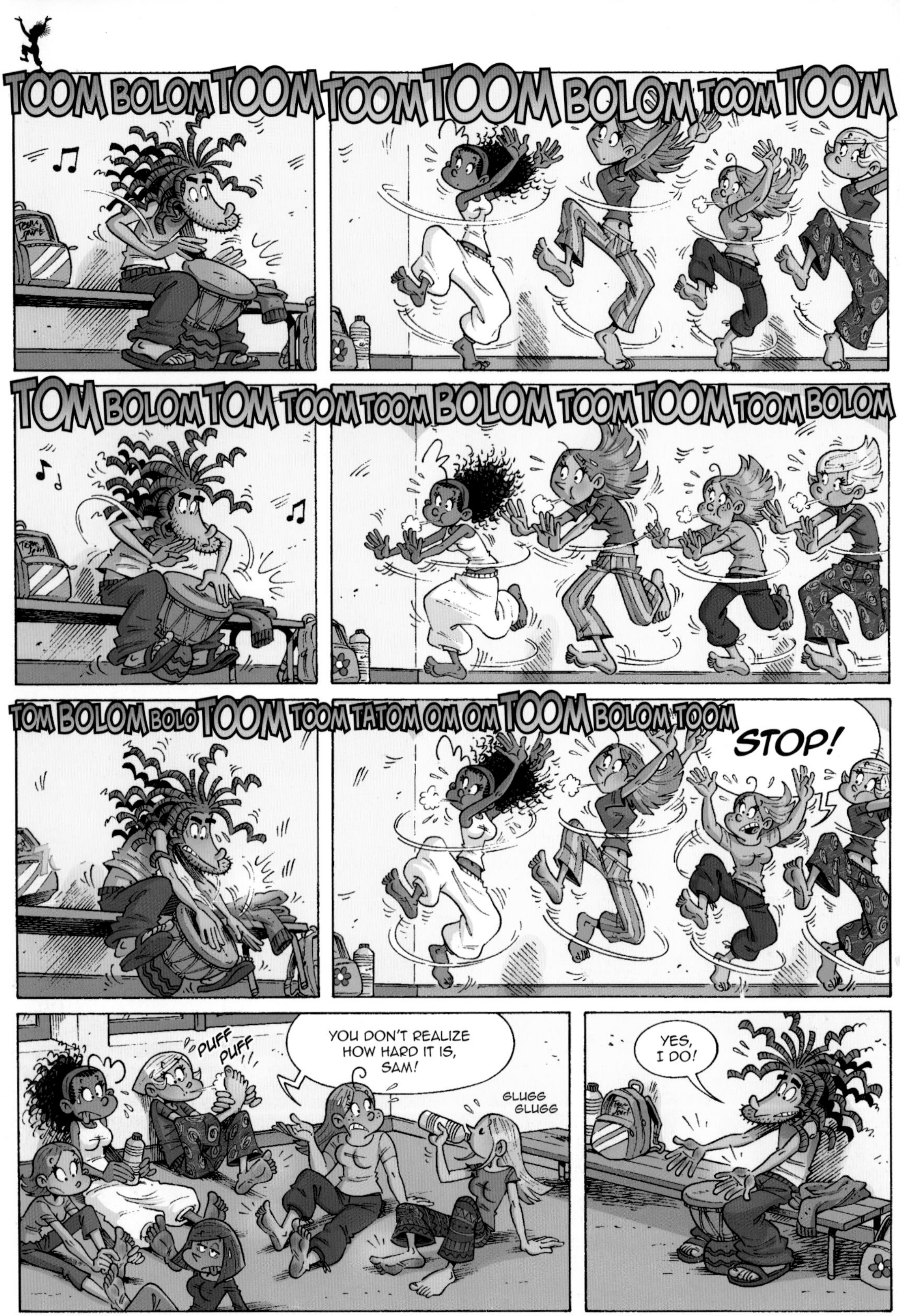
TOOM BOLOM TOOM TOOM TOOM BOLOM TOOM TOOM
TOM BOLOM TOM TOOM TOOM BOLOM TOOM TOOM TOOM BOLOM
TOM BOLOM BOLO TOOM TOOM TATOM OM OM TOOM BOLOM TOOM
STOP!
PUFF PUFF
YOU DON'T REALIZE HOW HARD IT IS, SAM!
GLUGG GLUGG
YES, I DO!

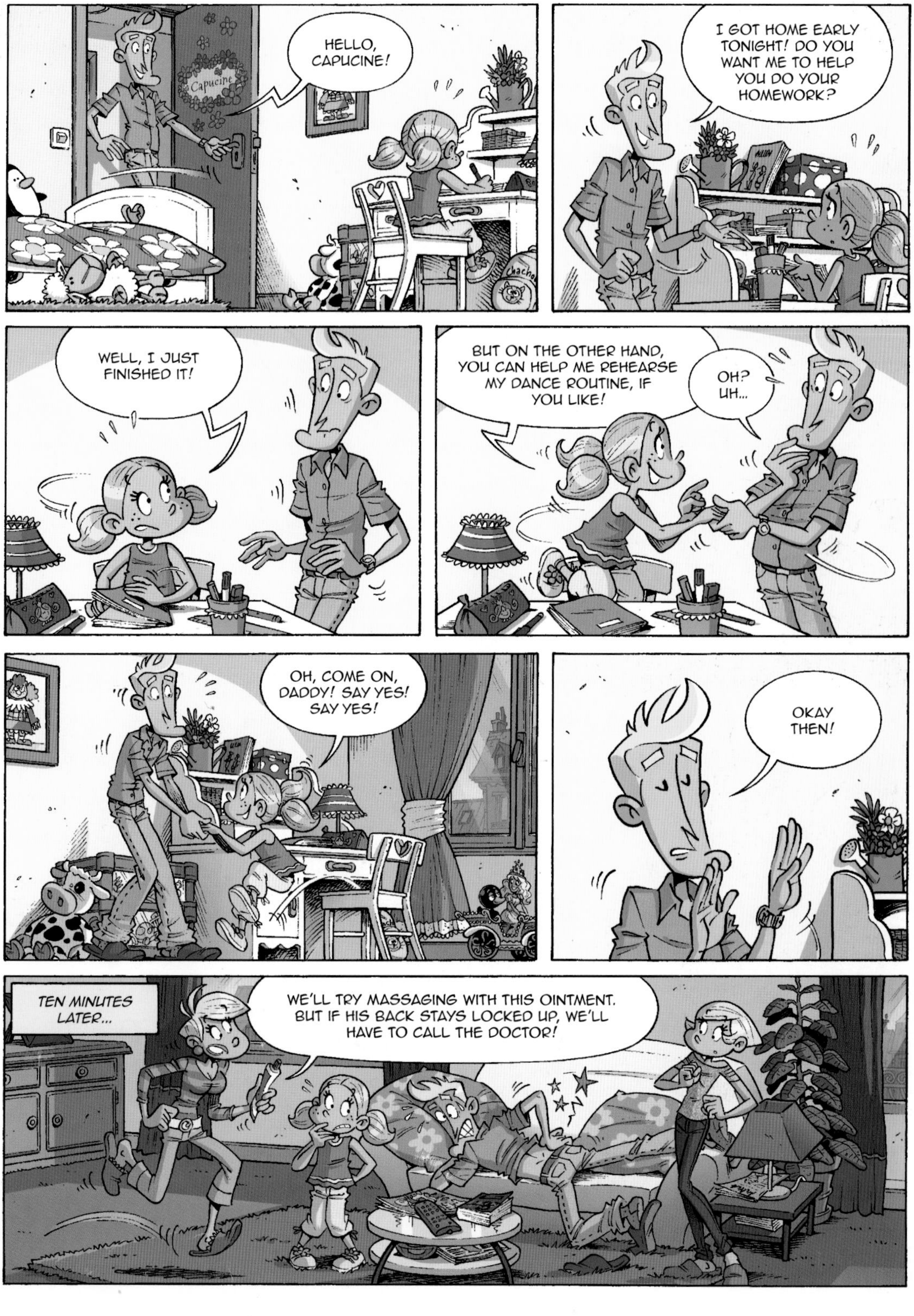
HELLO, CAPUCINE!
Capucine
I GOT HOME EARLY TONIGHT! DO YOU WANT ME TO HELP YOU DO YOUR HOMEWORK?
WELL, I JUST FINISHED IT!
BUT ON THE OTHER HAND, YOU CAN HELP ME REHEARSE MY DANCE ROUTINE, IF YOU LIKE!
OH? UH...
OH, COME ON, DADDY! SAY YES! SAY YES!
OKAY THEN!
TEN MINUTES LATER...
WE'LL TRY MASSAGING WITH THIS OINTMENT. BUT IF HIS BACK STAYS LOCKED UP, WE'LL HAVE TO CALL THE DOCTOR!

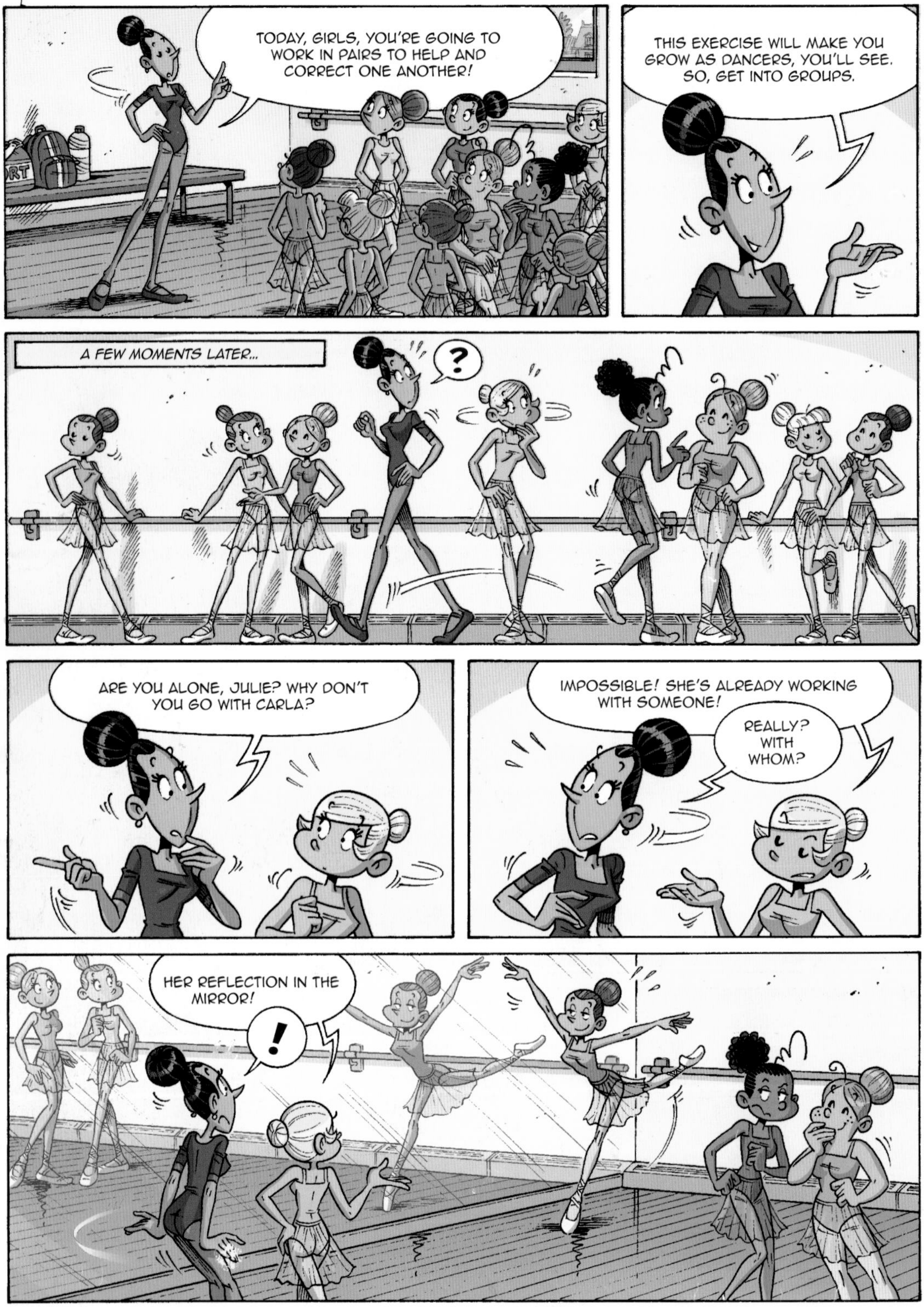
TODAY, GIRLS, YOU'RE GOING TO WORK IN PAIRS TO HELP AND CORRECT ONE ANOTHER!
THIS EXERCISE WILL MAKE YOU GROW AS DANCERS, YOU'LL SEE. SO, GET INTO GROUPS.
A FEW MOMENTS LATER...
?
ARE YOU ALONE, JULIE? WHY DON'T YOU GO WITH CARLA?
IMPOSSIBLE! SHE'S ALREADY WORKING WITH SOMEONE!
REALLY? WITH WHOM?
HER REFLECTION IN THE MIRROR!
!

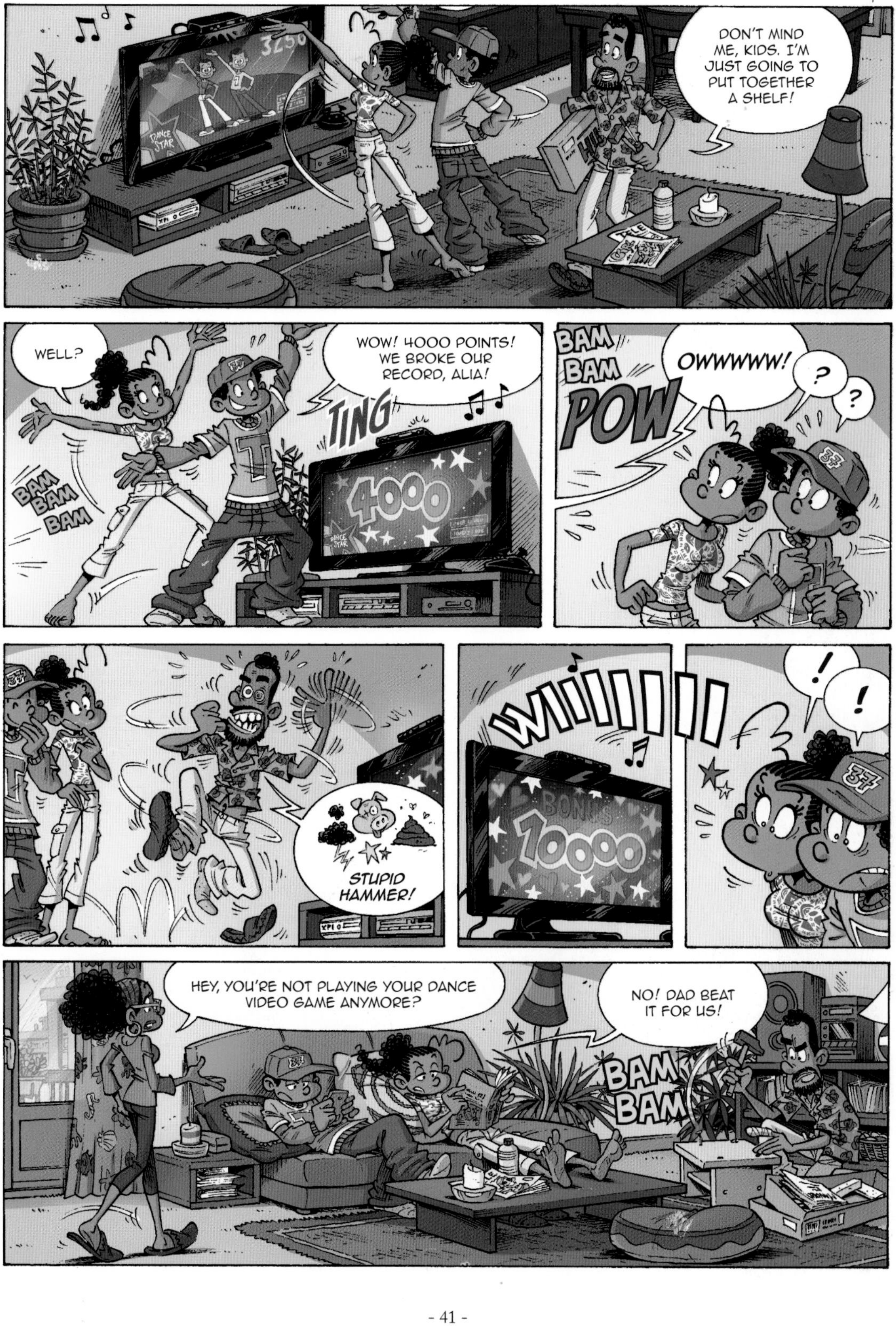
DON'T MIND ME, KIDS. I'M JUST GOING TO PUT TOGETHER A SHELF!
DANCE STAR
WELL?
WOW! 4000 POINTS! WE BROKE OUR RECORD, ALIA!
TING
BAM BAM BAM
4000
BAM BAM POW
OWWWWW!
?
?
STUPID HAMMER!
WIIIIIII
BONUS 10000
!
!
HEY, YOU'RE NOT PLAYING YOUR DANCE VIDEO GAME ANYMORE?
NO! DAD BEAT IT FOR US!
BAM BAM

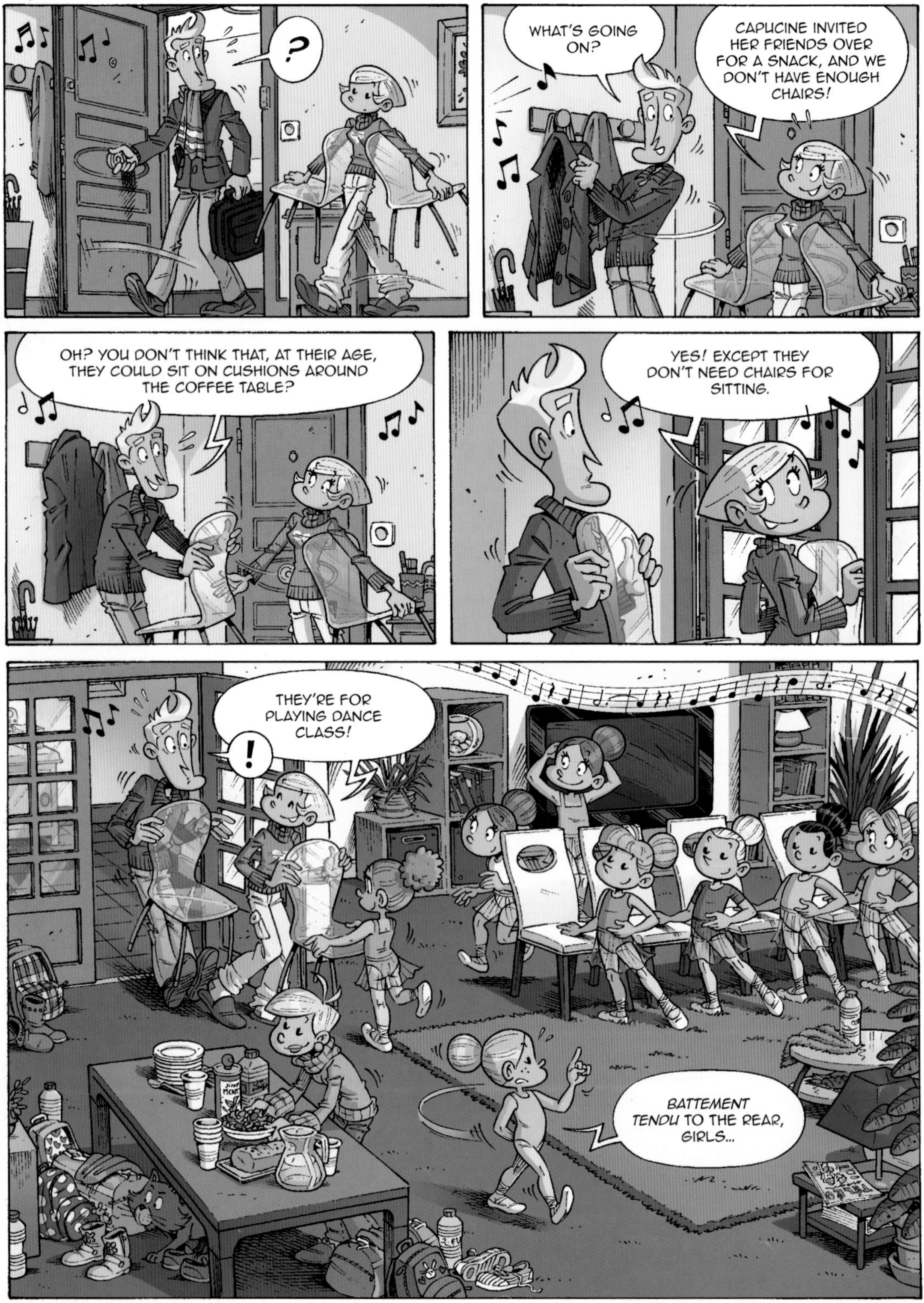
?
WHAT'S GOING ON?
CAPUCINE INVITED HER FRIENDS OVER FOR A SNACK, AND WE DON'T HAVE ENOUGH CHAIRS!
OH? YOU DON'T THINK THAT, AT THEIR AGE, THEY COULD SIT ON CUSHIONS AROUND THE COFFEE TABLE?
YES! EXCEPT THEY DON'T NEED CHAIRS FOR SITTING.
THEY'RE FOR PLAYING DANCE CLASS!
!
BATTEMENT TENDU TO THE REAR, GIRLS...

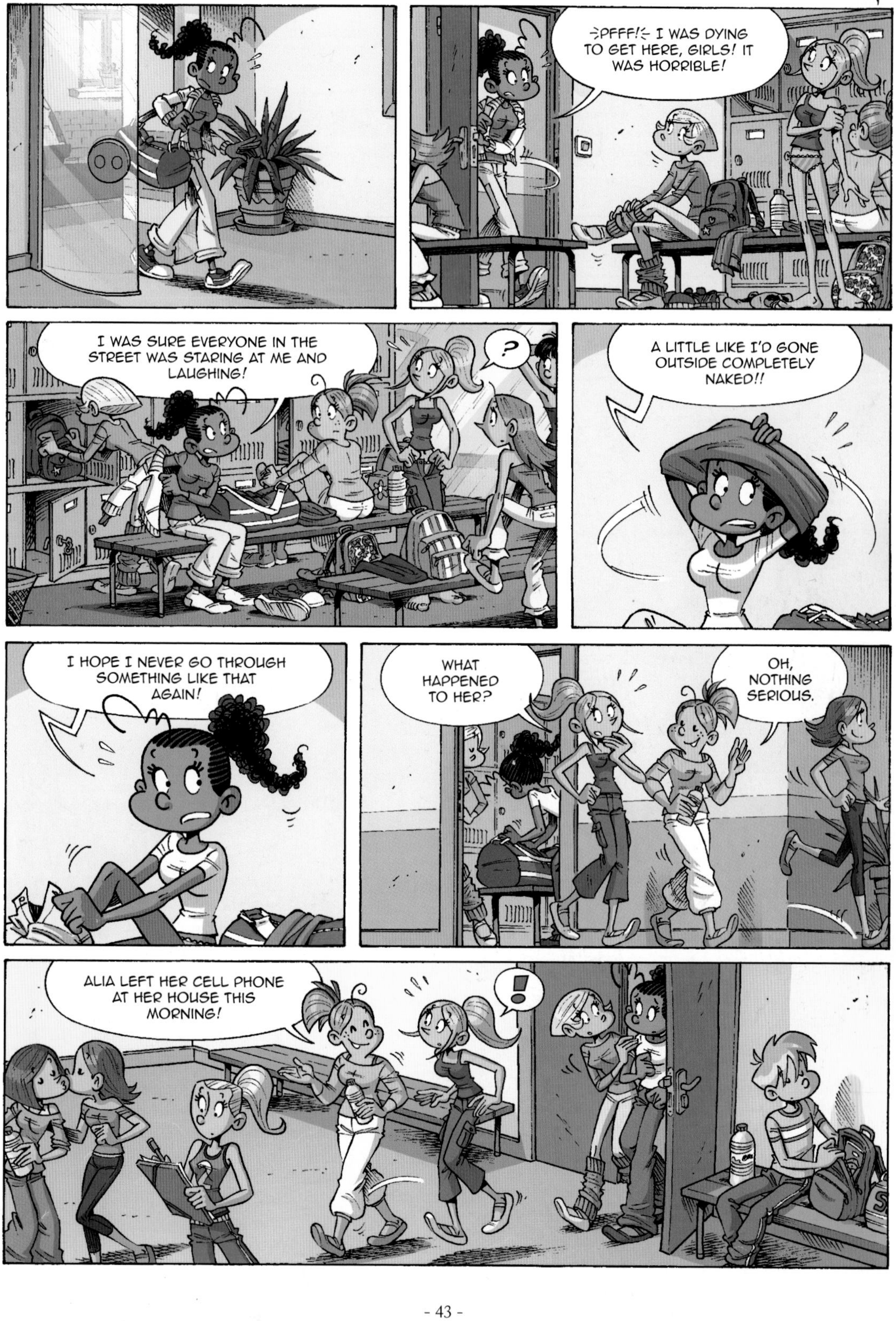

PFFF! I WAS DYING TO GET HERE, GIRLS! IT WAS HORRIBLE!
I WAS SURE EVERYONE IN THE STREET WAS STARING AT ME AND LAUGHING!
?
A LITTLE LIKE I'D GONE OUTSIDE COMPLETELY NAKED!!
I HOPE I NEVER GO THROUGH SOMETHING LIKE THAT AGAIN!
WHAT HAPPENED TO HER?
OH, NOTHING SERIOUS.
ALIA LEFT HER CELL PHONE AT HER HOUSE THIS MORNING!
!

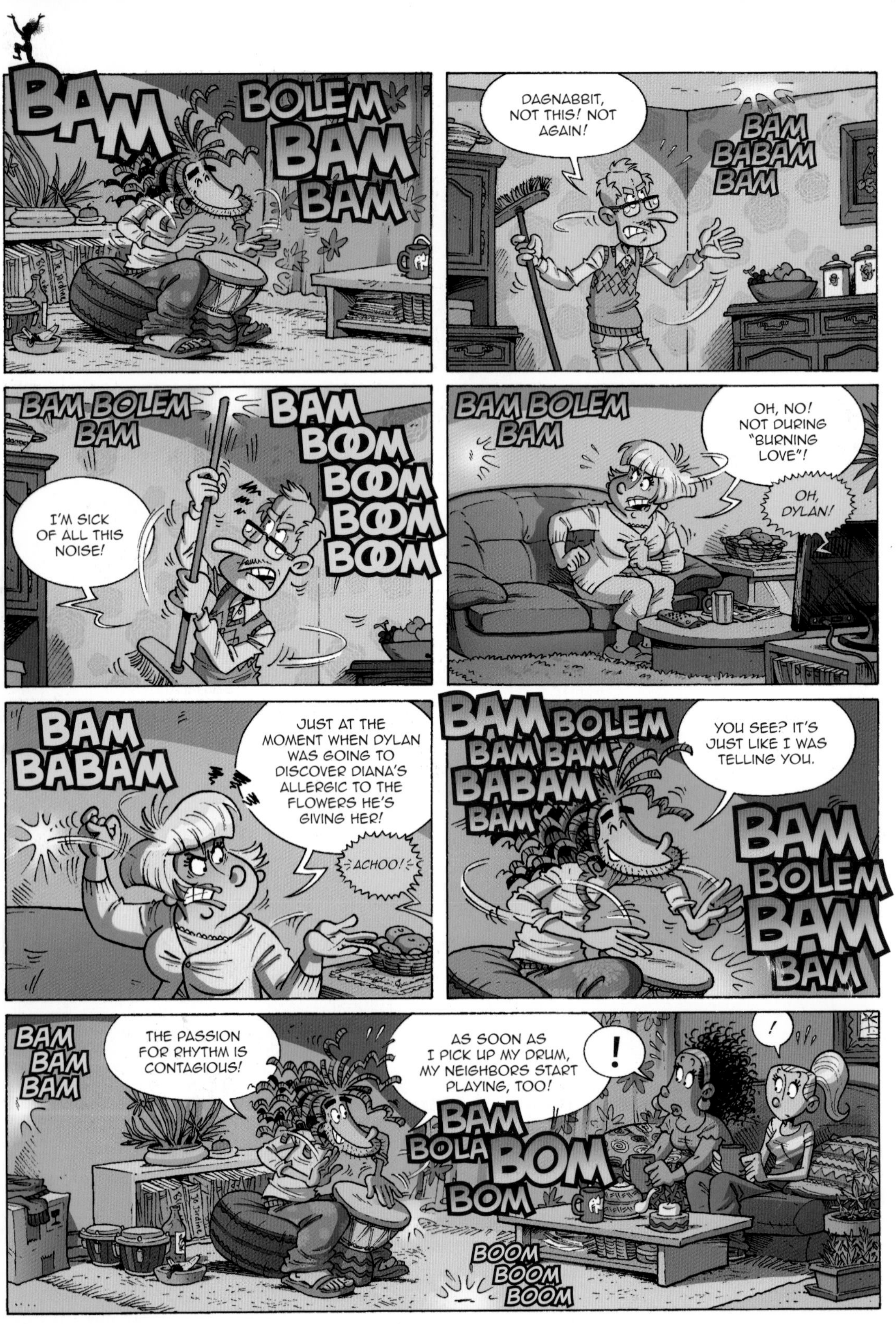

BAM
BOLEM BAM BAM
DAGNABBIT, NOT THIS! NOT AGAIN!
BAM BABAM BAM
BAM BOLEM BAM
BAM BOOM BOOM BOOM BOOM
I'M SICK OF ALL THIS NOISE!
BAM BOLEM BAM
OH, NO! NOT DURING "BURNING LOVE"!
OH, DYLAN!
BAM BABAM
JUST AT THE MOMENT WHEN DYLAN WAS GOING TO DISCOVER DIANA'S ALLERGIC TO THE FLOWERS HE'S GIVING HER!
ACHOO!
BAM BOLEM BAM BAM BABAM BAM
YOU SEE? IT'S JUST LIKE I WAS TELLING YOU.
BAM BOLEM BAM BAM
BAM BAM BAM
THE PASSION FOR RHYTHM IS CONTAGIOUS!
AS SOON AS I PICK UP MY DRUM, MY NEIGHBORS START PLAYING, TOO!
!
!
BAM BOLA BOM BOM
BOOM BOOM BOOM

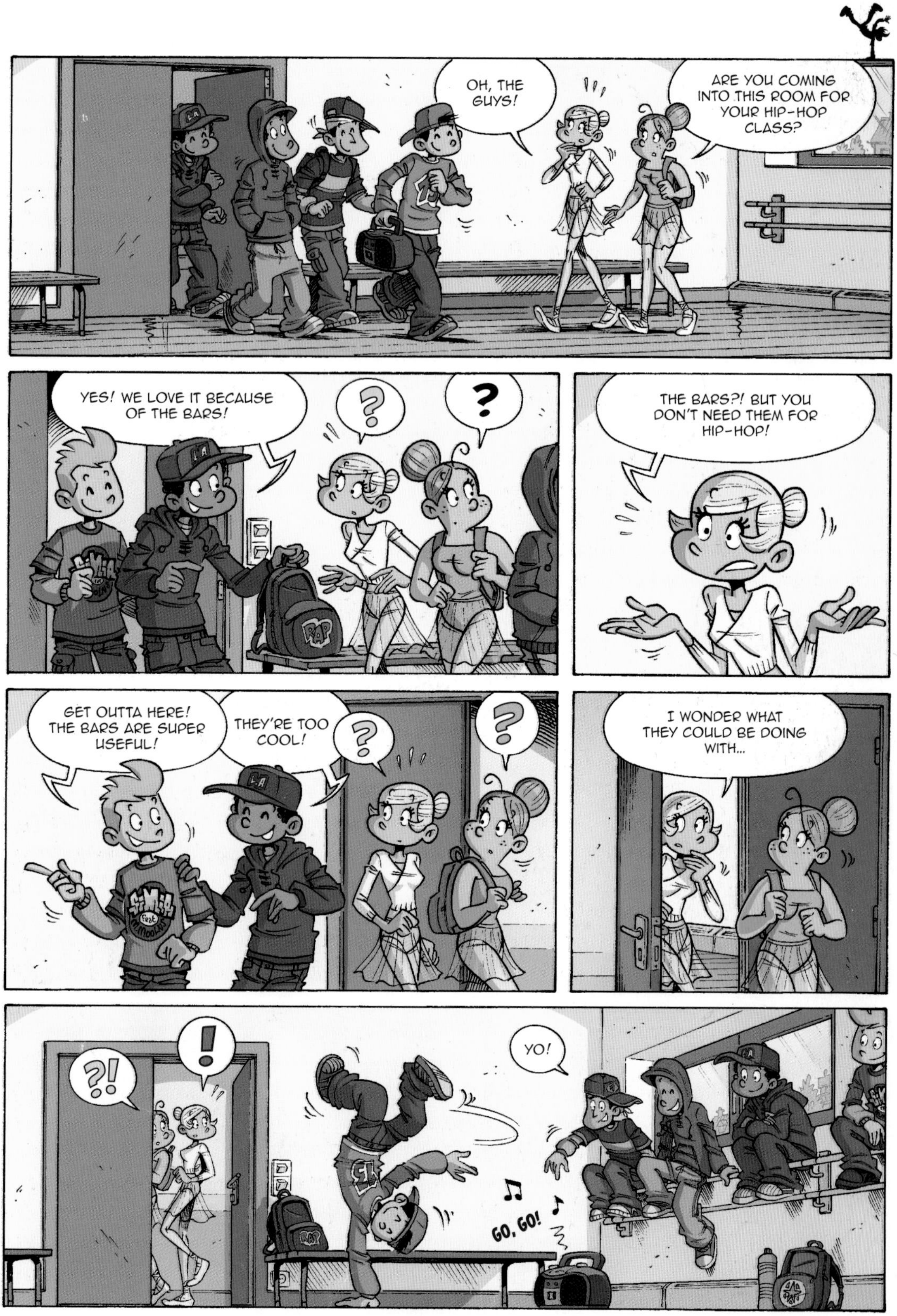
OH, THE GUYS!
ARE YOU COMING INTO THIS ROOM FOR YOUR HIP-HOP CLASS?
YES! WE LOVE IT BECAUSE OF THE BARS!
?
?
THE BARS?! BUT YOU DON'T NEED THEM FOR HIP-HOP!
GET OUTTA HERE! THE BARS ARE SUPER USEFUL!
THEY'RE TOO COOL!
?
?
I WONDER WHAT THEY COULD BE DOING WITH...
?!
!
YO!
GO, GO!

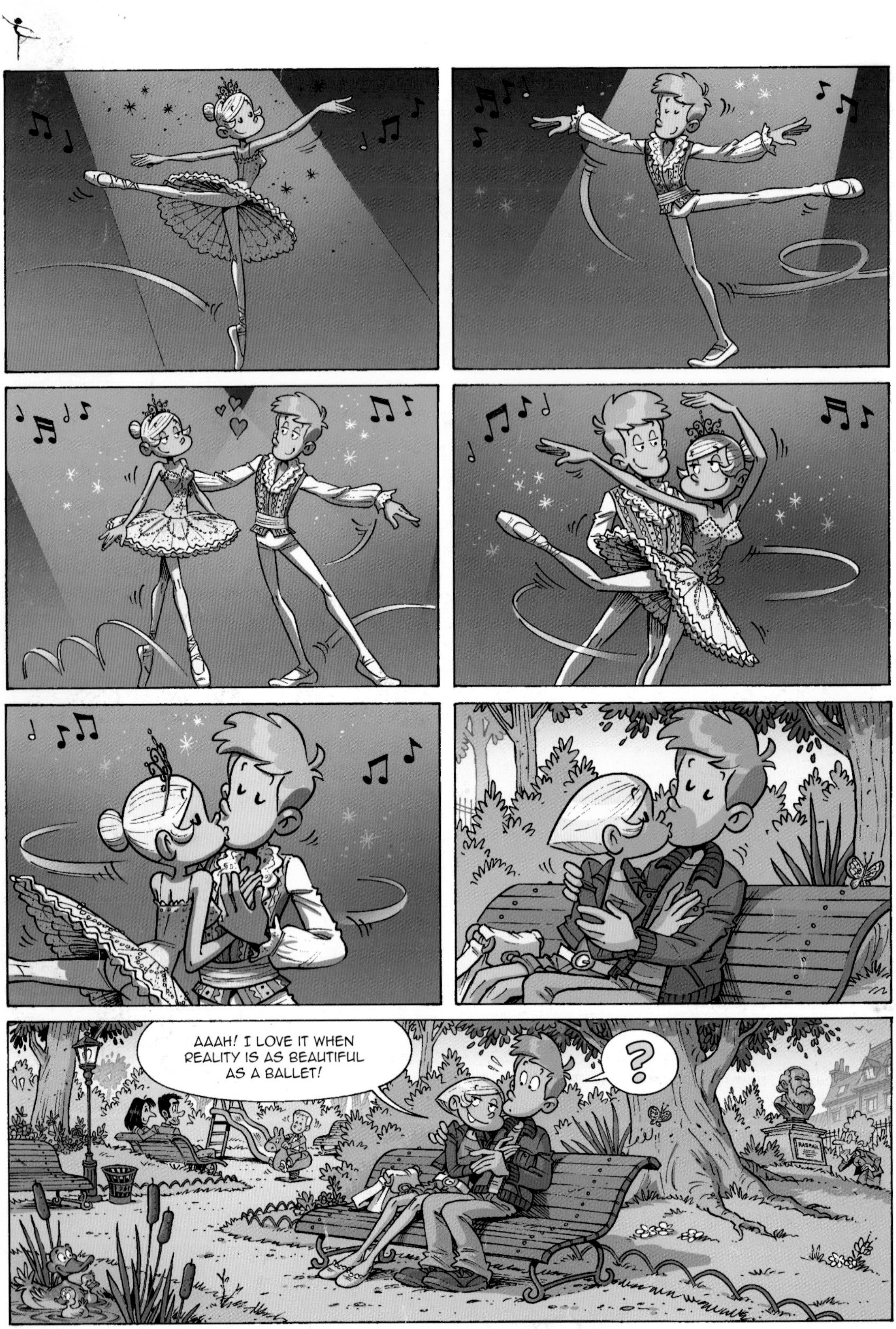
AAAH! I LOVE IT WHEN REALITY IS AS BEAUTIFUL AS A BALLET!
?
RASPAIL

WATCH OUT FOR PAPERCUTZ™

Welcome to the enticing, exciting, and enchanting eighth DANCE CLASS graphic novel by Crip & Béka, not to mention, Maëla Cosson, whose beautiful coloring is such an important part of DANCE CLASS. I'm Jim Salicrup, the Editor-in-Chief of Papercutz and unofficial eighth dwarf! All of us at Papercutz, while whistling while we work in our converted diamond mine, are dedicated to publishing great graphic novels for all ages. We hope you enjoy this and every DANCE CLASS graphic novel—we know we really enjoy them!

One of the great parts of my job at Papercutz is that I get to see all our awesome graphic novels before you do—and I even get paid for it! How cool is that? Here's a few that I think you may enjoy as well…

DISNEY FAIRIES #15 "Tinker Bell and the Secret of the Wings" – Who doesn't love Tinker Bell? Oh, sure she may have done a few questionable things in that *Peter Pan* movie, but she's a lot nicer now! In this particular graphic novel, we get to meet Tink's sister, but due to some very strange circumstances, no sooner do they finally meet, they then have to part—possibly forever! If that wasn't bad enough, an unfortunate accident threatens to destroy Pixie Hollow, the home of Tinker Bell and her fairy friends! You can't miss this one!

ERNEST & REBECCA #5 "The School of Nonsense" – I admit it—I just love ERNEST & REBECCA and I think you will too! Rebecca is a wonderful six-and-a-half year-old kid and Ernest is a microbe (or is he?). Normally, Ernest only appears to Rebecca when she is ill, but she's been very healthy lately. That may not last too long, as a nasty super zombie virus may infect everyone at her school. Please pick up an ERNEST & REBECCA graphic novel—these books are so brilliantly written and so beautifully drawn, I can't imagine anyone not loving each and every page!

Peyo
FOREVER SMURFETTE
PAPERCUTZ
© Peyo - 2014 - Licensed through Lafig Belgium - www.smurf.com

FOREVER SMURFETTE – This is a one-shot spin-off from our on-going series THE SMURFS. But let's face it, Smurfette is a real star and had to get a graphic novel of her own sooner or later! Among the stories contained in this all-new graphic novel is one we're sure you won't want to miss—Smurfette falls in love with an elf! But will that love endure when that elf betrays her to escape the clutches of Gargamel?

Of course, I'm sure you'll want to pick up the next DANCE CLASS graphic novel too, but as we go to press, we're not aware of what the story will be yet! That's why we suggest going to papercutz.com and looking for news and announcements about DANCE CLASS there, as well as info on everything else coming from Papercutz! So until next time, class dismissed!

Thanks,

JIM

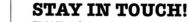

"A little silhouetto of a man"

STAY IN TOUCH!

EMAIL: salicrup@papercutz.com
WEB: papercutz.com
TWITTER: @papercutzgn
FACEBOOK: PAPERCUTZGRAPHICNOVELS
MAIL: Papercutz, 160 Broadway,
Suite 700, East Wing, New York, NY 10038

More Great Graphic Novels from PAPERCUTZ™

Tinker Bell
and the Secret of the Wings
PAPERCUTZ

DISNEY FAIRIES #15
"Tinker Bell and the Secret of the Wings"
The hit DVD in comics!

Guillaume Bianco
Antonello Dalena
Ernest & Rebecca
5
The School of Nonsense

ERNEST & REBECCA #5
"The School of Nonsense"
A 6 ½ year old girl and her microbial buddy against the world!

4 STORIES BASED UPON ORIGINAL CHARACTERS BY JIM DAVIS
the GARFIELD show
LITTLE TROUBLE IN BIG CHINA
PAPERCUTZ

THE GARFIELD SHOW #4
"Little Trouble in Big China"
As seen on the Cartoon Network!

Blue Sky Studios
RIO
SNAKES ALIVE!
PAPERCUTZ

RIO #1
"Snakes Alive!"
An all-new, exclusive prequel to RIO 2 that takes place after the original hit RIO film!

SMURFS
THE SMURF ACCOUNTANT
PAPERCUTZ

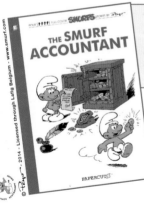

THE SMURFS #18
"The Smurf Accountant"
More money, more problems in the Smurf's Village!

SYBIL
the Backpack Fairy
4
"Princess Nina"
PAPERCUTZ

SYBIL THE BACKPACK FAIRY #4
"Princess Nina"
Nina and Sybil's Excellent Adventure Through Time!

Available at better booksellers everywhere!

Or order directly from us! DISNEY FAIRIES is available in paperback for $7.99, in hardcover for $11.99; ERNEST & REBECCA is $11.99 in hardcover only; THE GARFIELD SHOW is available in paperback for $7.99, in hardcover for $11.99; RIO is available in paperback for $7.99 each, in hardcover for $11.99; THE SMURFS are available in paperback for $5.99, in hardcover for $10.99; and SYBIL THE BACKPACK FAIRY is available in hardcover only for $10.99.

Please add $4.00 for postage and handling for the first book, add $1.00 for each additional book.

Please make check payable to NBM Publishing. Send to: PAPERCUTZ, 160 Broadway, Suite 700, East Wing, New York, NY 10038

(1-800-886-1223)

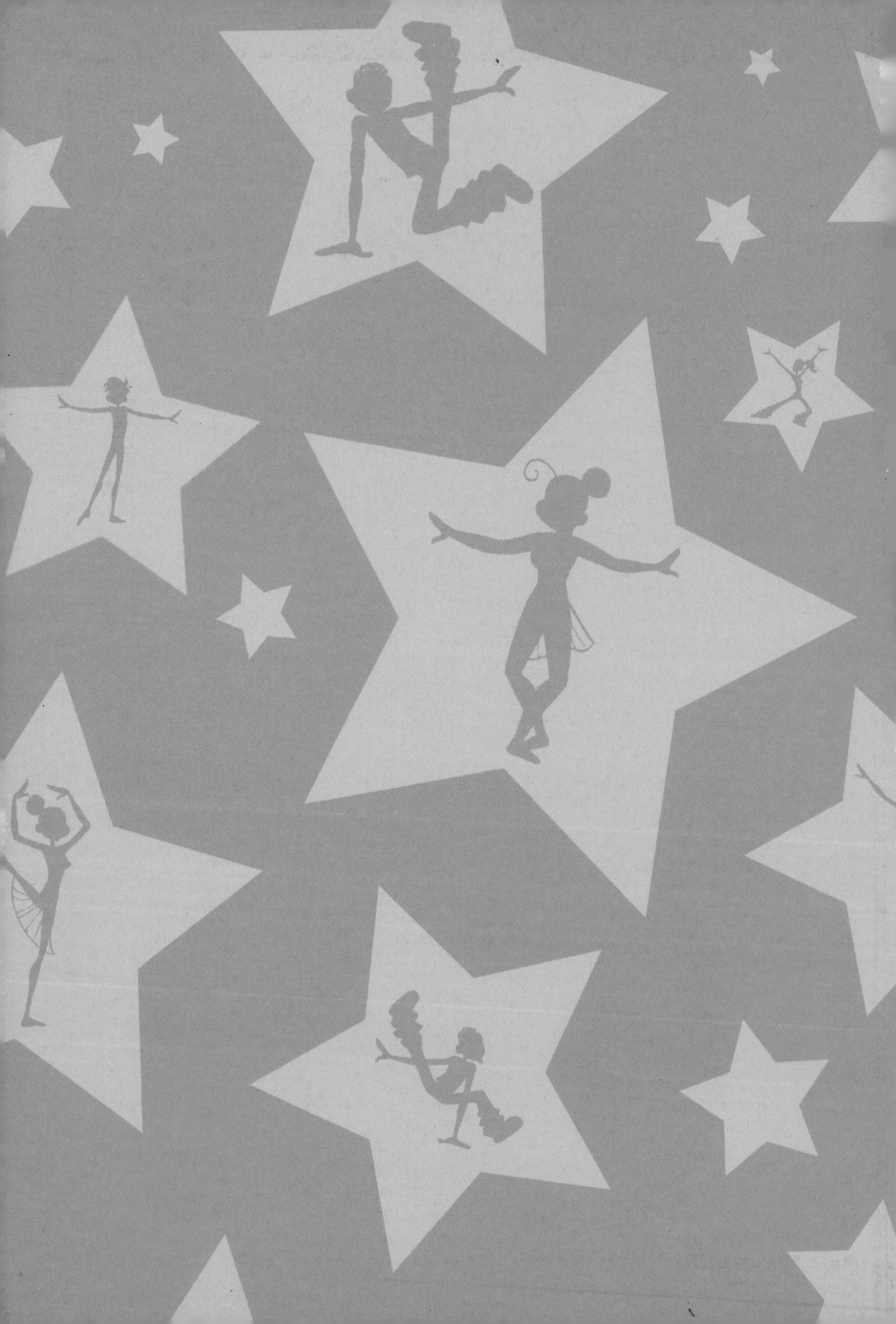